Another Batch of Warm Buns

Spanking short stories:
erotic, play and discipline

Susan Kohler

CCB Publishing
British Columbia, Canada

Another Batch of Warm Buns: Spanking short stories: erotic, play and discipline

Copyright ©2007 by Susan Kohler
ISBN-13 978-0-9783893-4-5
First Edition

Library and Archives Canada Cataloguing in Publication

Kohler, Susan, 1950-
Another Batch of Warm Buns: spanking short stories: erotic, play and discipline / written by Susan Kohler. – 1st ed.
Also available in electronic format.
ISBN 978-0-9783893-4-5
1. Sexual dominance and submission--Fiction. 2. Sadomasochism--Fiction. 3. Corporal punishment--Fiction. I. Title.
PS3611.O47A65 2007 813'.6 C2007-904608-8

Publisher: CCB Publishing
             British Columbia, Canada
             www.ccbpublishing.com

Dedication

This one is for my friends in the spanking scene, especially the ones who come to my parties, or who go to the parties one county over because you guys are simply the best people I know, weird, yes, but the best people I know.

Other books by Susan Kohler

The Paddle Club

Hot Crossed Buns

The Heart of the Beast

Preface

This book, like *Hot Crossed Buns*, grew out of my experiences and imagination but also well, a sense of desperation. I had too many stories for one book, and decided to split them in two.

The funny thing is once I got the idea to write more, the story ideas came. I've mixed the spanking that I call 'fun' with the ones I call 'discipline.' The difference is easy to see; if the bottom wants to be spanked, that's fun. If the bottom is being spanked to teach him or her a lesson, that's discipline. Sometimes, as in real life, the fun spankings are pretty severe.

Contents

1. You Bet Your Ass 9

2. Jesse: The Hard-Handed Janitor 25

3. Personal: Command Performance 39

4. The Lash Resort Ranch 50

5. Spanked By Email 66

6. A Painful Lesson 74

7. Personal: One Tough Customer 88

8. Cindy's Spanking 100

9. Mucho Macho Man 107

10. It's Never Too Late 118

11. She's No Angel 135

12. C.O.P.S.: Count On Painful Smacks 148

Author's Note 180

One

You Bet Your Ass

How about betting something other than money on sports? Say, for instance spankings? A swat per run in baseball is one thing but a swat per point in football could be painful (especially if the game is one-sided), and I don't even want to think about basketball. Also, both sexes could get it, got it?

Christie Larsen squirmed as she sat on the padded barstool. Her tan linen slacks felt somehow tighter than they should, her shapely buttocks were tingling and sensitive. She ran her fingers nervously through her tousled blond hair. They were watching the football game in the bar with friends, but she wasn't really a football fan. The reason she was so antsy, was that she had picked the wrong team to bet on. Her team was losing and losing badly. The game was almost over.

She and her lover, Randy Finley, had given new meaning to the phrase, *"You bet your ass!"* That was exactly what they'd bet and it looked like she was going to pay the bet with just that piece of her anatomy, her ass. Trying not to squirm, she asked herself how she had gotten into such a predicament. She ignored the game as she thought back to the start of the baseball season, back to the start of the private bets between herself and Randy.

It had been a warm afternoon in May, she and Randy had spent the morning in bed making slow, lazy love. Then they took a shower that probably wasted more water than they should have, with the drought in California. They went out to a champagne brunch, then hurried home in time for the baseball game.

Christie hated baseball almost as much as she loved Randy, so she had resigned herself to a long, boring afternoon. The things

9

she did for the love of her man she thought, looking at Randy. It's almost a shame he's so beautiful. She stretched out on the sofa and studied his handsome, chiseled face, his muscular build, his blue eyes and shoulder length black hair. He was sitting beside her on the sofa waiting for the start of the game, stroking her hips and ass.

"God, I love your butt," he said. "I love stroking and kissing it." He hesitated, "There's only one thing I'd love to do more with it."

"What's that?" Christie thought she knew. "Are you asking me to try sodomy again?"

Randy had convinced her to try sodomy, but she didn't really like it. It was too painful with Randy's large cock.

"Okay, two things. The one you don't know about is," he leaned over to kiss her mouth and then whispered in her ear, "I'd like to spank your beautiful butt, very slowly and very, very hard."

"What?" Christie was surprised, her brilliant blue eyes wide as she asked, "Spank me! Why? Why would you want to hurt me? What have I ever done to you?"

This was something she had never thought of letting any man do to her.

"I don't want to hurt you. I would never, ever hurt you," Randy protested. "Hurting you has nothing to do with it. A friendly, sexy, little spanking isn't going to hurt. Sting maybe. Smart a little, maybe. But not hurt."

"Yeah, that part about spanking me very hard doesn't sound like it would hurt at all," she sneered. "Why would it?"

"It wouldn't hurt. It would just sting." Randy seemed to think that he was making sense, but somehow Christie doubted his logic.

"I think your ass is one of the first things I was attracted to about you. I mean, I love your wavy, long blonde hair, your bright blue eyes and you have a fantastic shape. Your breasts are full and just the right size, large but not too large. I love your personality too," he said earnestly, wanting her to understand. "You're intelligent and warm and funny. But it was your ass that got my attention first when I saw you bending over, trying to get that kid's baseball out from under your car. Without seeing anything else of you, I wanted to go out with you. I love your ass. I've always wanted to spank it and to see it turn pink, then red, and get warm. Then, when it's nice and hot and stings a bit, I want to make hard, passionate love to you, really pound you into the mattress. It'd be fun."

Randy continued, "I would never do it unless you were willing, and I would always quit when you said to stop. You could trust me, you know that, but I would always want you to be willing to submit. To roll over and uncover your butt, then wait for me to slap it and make it turn bright pink and smart."

"So what brought this up?" Christie asked suspiciously. "Now, I mean. Why did you decide to play *True Confessions* just before a baseball game? Is this a sort of plot to get me to watch the damn game without complaining? Am I being distracted or is this a real decision? Is the choice between baseball and a spanking? Baseball sounds like the safer of the two." She narrowed her eyes and stared at him, "Come on, Randy, I know you had a reason for bringing this up at this exact moment, what is it?"

"Can't fool you, huh?" Randy almost looked a little guilty, almost. "All right, I was thinking of making a bet, a fun little bet with you about the game. It would make it more interesting for you to watch." This last part sounded hopeful and yet a bit devious. "Then I remembered how you always say *you bet your ass,'* so I figured why not? We could bet swats on each other's butt. At first, just as an experiment. Later, if you like it, maybe in the future, we can up the wagers a little bit, but never more than you want to bet. Never."

Christie considered his words for a moment, looking into Randy's smiling, mischievous face, then arched an eyebrow and said, "So? It's worse than I thought. It's not a choice between doing one of two things I don't really want to do, just to please you. You want to have it both ways. You want me to watch a baseball game, which I think is boring, and have a spanking! Which sounds painful. Fine! Great!" Her voice didn't sound like she thought it was fine or great.

"You could win the bet, you know," Randy grinned, "then you'd get to spank me."

"That's a thought," she mused, then went on, "okay, I'll consider it. Spell out the terms and remember, if you lose the bet I'll get to give the swats to you!"

Amazing, she thought, how far she would be willing to go to make a baseball game exciting! Even more amazing was how far she would go to please Randy. It's a good thing he's worth it.

"Okay. Here's what I was thinking. At the end of each inning the person betting on the team losing at that point, gets a swat on the butt for every run that their team is behind. Not on the bare butt and not really hard. Okay, so far?"

Christie nodded, thinking that it didn't sound too bad, yet. She had never really been spanked but several men had slapped her on the ass before. Is it something about her behind? Does it have a bulls-eye on it that only men can see? She wondered.

Randy went on. "After the swats from the last inning of the game, the loser gets a swat for all the runs scored by both teams, bare bottom and much harder. All right? Remember, you could win. I could be the one who gets most of the swats."

Somehow, Christie decided as she listened to Randy, this bet sounded pretty well thought out. It was not just an off-the-cuff idea. She had never been spanked by anyone, not even as a child, but she didn't think this sounded too terrible. Baseball games usually have such low scores. Heck, half the time the scores were 1-0, or 2-1.

Christie considered the idea for a little while, then she nodded. "Okay we'll try it once, and if I don't like it, that's the end of it. What if we both want to pick the same team?"

"We'll cut cards for it." They shook on the bet just as the game started.

The first game seemed a little bizarre to Christie, her team was leading 1-0 at the end of the first inning but she found it hard to give Randy the swat on his butt. She had never thought of hitting him or anyone else. Not really.

When the score remained unchanged at the end of the second inning, Randy grabbed her hand.

He said, "Come on, Christie, don't be such a wimp. You hit like a girl. Hit me a little harder please, put some force into it. When it's my turn to swat your butt, I sure will!" She gave his ass a fairly decent swat and he said, "Better, but you still hit like a girl."

Christie protested, "But I *am* a girl!"

"That's no excuse!" Randy laughed, dodging the pillow that Christie threw at him.

Just then, Randy's team had a batter hit a home run with two men on. "Oh my God!" she exclaimed. "You're going to hit me this time."

When the inning ended Randy looked at her and asked, "Going to wimp out?"

Randy made some funny chicken clucks but stopped when Christie rolled over and waited for him to give her the swats. He gave her butt two hard, sharp slaps, one on each cheek.

"I love to keep things balanced out," he explained. "Now did that hurt?"

Reluctantly she admitted, "No, I'll admit that it didn't hurt, I hardly felt it."

"It feels pretty good, I'll bet." He gave her a knowing smile.

"Yeah, sure." She was sarcastic. "But don't tell my lover because he's a sadist." She cuddled up in Randy's arms.

During the next inning she found out that Randy could watch baseball and kiss at the same time, and very well too. Christie got two more swats at the end of the fourth inning but the score was tied at the end of the fifth. By the sixth inning, she found out that Randy could also suck on a tit and watch baseball, although he almost bit her nipple off when there was a great play! She led by one at the end of the sixth, and this time she laid it on him pretty hard.

At the end of the seventh she got to give him another swat, and at the end of the eighth her lead was two. At the end of the ninth inning the game was tied. In the tenth, disaster struck as she lost 6-5. Eleven swats, bare bottom, and much harder! Christie stared at Randy, her eyes big and round.

Randy gave her the single swat for the tenth inning before he gave her the quiet, firm command, "Zipper, love."

Reluctantly, she unzipped her jeans and rolled over. She raised her hips to let Randy pull the jeans off her butt and slide her lacy panties down. She waited nervously for him to give her the harder swats on her bare bottom. Which he did, with a vengeance; all eleven were sharp and unmerciful. Each sharp slap made Christie squirm and gasp. They were a lot harsher than the previous swats, but strangely enough she didn't really mind, not at all.

He rolled her over, and Rick, not being one to waste an open zipper, lowered his mouth to her soft, moist pussy.

"So," she managed to say to Randy between moans, "is this when the part about pounding me into the mattress starts?"

"No, it starts after the next game. Which team do you want to bet on this time?"

"God! You really *are* a sadist." She managed to get the words out before he lowered his head again, making it hard for her to think, let alone answer. "You want me to watch *two* baseball games and also let you spank me hard?"

They picked teams and watched a second game.

Christie started to enjoy their private bet a little bit more this time, even though for each of the first three innings she got one sharp swat. For the next three innings Randy got two swats each inning. Then for two innings it was tied. The game ended with her giving him seven swats on his bare ass, and she gave them quite vigorously. She had finally gotten completely into the spirit of the bet.

As Randy had promised, he took her into the bedroom and made love to her, a rough passionate kind of lovemaking that really fit his prediction of pounding her into the mattress. He spent a lot of time just teasing her, arousing her, sucking her pussy. He raised himself up above her and thrust into her soft, warm cunt. He started slowly and built it up into a crashing explosion. They both noticed that, if anything, the sex was a little wilder and more uninhibited after the light spankings.

The baseball season went on, with each one getting their share of playful spankings. Christie began to like it even though the spankings got a little harder each time. The sex that almost invariably followed got a little wilder each time too.

When football season started they carried on the bets, but only on pro football, not college. They altered the terms, too. They bet swats at the end of the half, over the clothes for the points scored by the opposing team. At the end of the game, the person betting on the losing team got bare-bottom swats for the total points margin. The swats became harder still, and the scores were higher. Then they started betting on the game by quarters.

They also started using a small cutting board of Christie's as a paddle. It had a rectangular shape, about 4 x 6 inches, and was about half an inch thick; there was a wooden handle and a 4 x 4-inch tile set into the surface. The tile had a rooster painted on it. It stung like hell and made a noisy crack when it came into sharp contact with bare buttocks, but left no marks or permanent damage. The two gamblers both got their share of harder and longer spankings. They only bet on games that they could watch at home, together. Then they could settle up at each quarter and the half, and at the end of the game without waiting to get home from watching the game. The football season was highlighted by red-hot bottoms and hotter sex.

There was an exception to the pattern. They bet on one college game; to them, it was the only college game. It was an old traditional cross-town rivalry in southern California. They didn't bet by the half or quarters, it was all out on the final score, but it was on total points scored by both teams. The spanking could be given in any way, with any kind of paddle or strap, in any place the winner wished. Christie lost 17-10, for a total of 27 swats.

Randy had Christie get a short length of rope which he used to tie her hands to the showerhead.

Seeing his intentions, Christie gave a nervous little laugh, "You're going to *tie* me to the showerhead, how Marquis De Sade of you."

"That's not all." He pulled out a square of black silk cloth. "I'm going to blindfold you too."

"Oh no, you're not," Christie protested.

"Oh yes, I am." Randy mocked her assertively.

He tied the scrap of silk over her eyes then turned on the water, and with her shower gel he soaped her ass. He played with the lather then turned off the shower and untied her without rinsing the lather off. He had her turn so that her butt was facing the open side of the shower stall, then had her spread her legs as far apart as the stall allowed. He told her to bend as far over as she could, bracing her hands on the tiled wall and sticking her butt out.

Instead of finding something new to hit her with, he used their old favorite paddle to settle the bet. He started to administer the swats, which he delivered quite a bit more energetically than ever before. Each blow was spaced out so that she could feel the pain separately, and each one was given with a hard fast stroke. They really stung her soapy white ass. She gasped and moaned all through the spanking, but only screamed once.

He turned on the warm water and rinsed the soap off her bright pink ass. Then he turned the water off again. He sat on the high step that formed the entrance to the shower stall. Taking her hips into his hands, he began to kiss and lick her butt, her anus, and ducking his head a little, her pussy. Finally, he joined her in the shower, turning the water back on. He had her get on her knees and suck his cock. He stopped her before he came and, bracing her back to the wall, lifted her onto his erect cock. He held her with his strong hands, firmly and not very gently squeezing her sore butt. It was fantastic! The bonus was that they managed all the athletic screwing without breaking their necks!

So it continued until the pro playoffs started. The local team was in the playoffs, and they felt it was even more exciting to watch the game with friends. That's when they decided they could go out to watch the game and still settle the bets afterwards, at home. They went to the sports bar and watched the game with their friends Bill and Vicki.

At the end of the first quarter, Christie's team led 3-0. She made a note on her napkin. "That's three to you, Randy," she said with an evil laugh. "Is there someplace around here where we can settle up?"

"I don't think so. Let's wait until we get home," he suggested.

"Then I get to give you what you have coming."

"Don't worry love, you'll get some too," Randy replied with a smile and a pinch on her fanny. "In fact, my team just scored a touchdown!"

He threw her a wink and a pat on the same spot that he had just pinched.

"Come on, what's the bet you two?" Bill asked. "I'm confused, when Christie's team scores, she states that Randy is going to get something. Then, when Randy's team scores, Christie is going to get some. Some what?"

"It's personal," Randy answered, while Christie blushed and choked on her drink. "Christie would kill me if I told you."

"You mean it's a sexy bet?" Bill persisted. "Come on Christie, are you too chicken to tell us about it? I dare you!"

Christie knew Bill, knew he was curious, knew he was persistent, knew he would keep up with the steady questioning until he found out the answer. She studied him for a moment, staring intently at his brown eyes and his warm, cheerful round face. Finally she seemed to come to a decision.

She downed her drink in one swallow and blurted out, "We bet our asses!"

"What do you mean?" Vicki asked.

"Spankings! We bet swats on the butt, one for each point ahead, by the quarter, and total score at the end of the game," Christie told the pair, blushing furiously. "I get to give him three swats for the three point lead my team had at the end of the first quarter. So far he gets to give me four at the half. God! Make that ten, no eleven!" she exclaimed as his team scored and made the extra point.

"Kinda makes the ole ass feel warm all over already, doesn't it love?" Randy patted her butt.

"You beat her?" Vicki was shocked. She shook her head sending her short brown curls springing.

"No, he doesn't beat me, just playful little spankings. Besides, sometimes I win and I get to paddle his butt!" Christie tried to reassure her friend.

The score remained 14-3 at the half, so it was three to Randy and eleven to Christie. They waited for the second half kickoff. The third quarter was aggravating for both of them as both of the teams threatened, but nobody scored.

Their friends, Bill and Vicki, got caught up in the bet. Bill began to cheer for Randy's team, although he was usually for the other side, and Vicki started cheering for Christie's. She really didn't give a damn which team won, but she was horrified at the very idea of Christie getting a spanking.

Finally with 1:37 left in the third quarter, Christie's team scored making it 14-10. Then they recovered a fumble right after the kickoff and scored again making it 14-17. The third quarter ended with the tally for quarterly swats being six to Randy, eleven to Sally, and so far thirty-one for whoever lost at the end of the game.

In the fourth quarter, Randy's team came to life and scored two touchdowns, making it 28-17. The final tally was six to Randy and twenty-two to Christie, for the quarters. Then, a walloping forty-five to Christie with the paddle on her bare butt for the points both teams had scored by the end of the game!

"Randy, you can't give her that many, you'll really hurt her!" Vicki protested. "Twenty-two swats is bad enough, but forty-five more for the total score. That's sixty-seven swats!"

"No Vicki, twenty-two swats with his hand and forty-five blows with the paddle! Christie can take it. She can trust me not to hurt her. Not too much, anyway." Randy enjoyed Vicki's obvious state of horror and fascination. It was one of the most interesting combination of emotions that he had ever seen on anyone's face! "Relax, it's only a bet on a game. It's not like we're talking real hardcore S & M."

Christie leaned over to whisper in Vicki's ear. Vicki went red but she didn't make any more protests.

"So? What'd you say to her?" Randy asked on the drive home.

"I told her that you wouldn't really hurt me because you wanted to fuck my brains out as soon as it was all over!" Christie laughed. "What do you want to bet that they have a little wager between themselves for next week's playoff game?"

When they got back to Christie's house, they found out that Bill and Vicki had followed them home. The other couple had a strange request.

"Please, can we watch while you settle your bets?" Bill asked. "I know it's a lot to ask. It's private and personal, and probably more than a little embarrassing, but Vicki's worried about Christie. You know how she is, I'll never get another moment's rest. Also, to be truthful, I'm a little curious."

"It's okay with me as long as it's okay with Christie," Randy said, as usual he was agreeable to almost anything. "But I don't think you'll be able to convince her."

Christie moved closer to Randy and whispered in his ear. She whispered for a long, long time. Randy grinned and nodded. She spoke to the waiting couple.

"A little bit curious, Bill? Get real! If you were a cat, as in curiosity killed the..., you'd be dead," she laughed at him.

She looked at Vicki, squarely meeting her best friend's warm brown eyes. "Will you take my word for it? It's going to be okay." She read the answer in Vicki's face and laughed. "Okay, come on in as long as you leave before we get to the part where Randy fucks my brains out. But there's a price."

"What price?" Vicki asked with trepidation.

"You'll find out." Randy winked at her, "Believe me, you'll find out."

They all went into the house. When Christie got inside, she laid on the sofa, face down.

"Go to it, Randy!" she said cheerfully.

He gave her the twenty-two swats, very hard, smart and fast. Each swat made a muffled THUNK as it landed on her slacks.

She got up and Randy bent over on the end of the sofa and got his six swats.

Speaking quietly to Randy, Christie said, "Remember your promise."

Vicki was exclaiming over the spanking she had witnessed. She didn't even notice that Randy, standing partly behind her had raised his eyebrows and got Bill's attention. He swung his head and gave a pointed look at Vicki's butt, then he looked back at Bill. He raised his eyebrows again with a big questioning grin on his face. Bill gave a slight nod. Bill made his way around to the front of Vicki and then grabbed her in a bear hug.

He said, "Go for it!"

Randy gave Vicki a spanking exactly like the one Christie had received, very hard and smart. It was fast, sharp, and lasted for twenty-two swats. When it was over, Bill released Vicki.

Then Randy politely asked, "Coffee, anyone?"

At their nods, he went in to make some.

It was funny to watch Vicki. She was so mad she was sputtering, but she was also surprised and exasperated. At least it finally made her shut up. Christie was sitting on the sofa next to Bill, and they were both laughing hysterically. Randy brought out some coffee, some cold cuts and Swiss cheese that he sliced on a small cutting board. He went to the kitchen when he realized that he had forgotten the cream and sugar. He served the refreshments.

After several minutes passed he asked in a casual tone of voice, "So Vicki, how does your butt feel?"

Vicki said, "What?" Then she realized what he meant. "It doesn't hurt!" She was genuinely surprised.

"I'm sorry we had to ambush you like that. It seemed to be the only way to convince you that I wasn't about to be beaten to death," Christie said.

"But won't the paddle hurt more?" Vicki asked.

"Yes, but not enough to really matter. It really just stings enough to make it a little scarier and more exciting. Understand now?" Christie asked.

"I guess so," she grinned ruefully. "I'd better try to understand. Or else I might get a surprise demo of the paddle. Do you really get to paddle Randy sometimes?" She secretly thought it might even be fun to paddle Bill.

"She sure does, and she's ruthless," Randy replied. "But now it *is* time for the paddle. I really hate to say this Vicki, but you are definitely going to get a demo of the paddle. In fact, this time I think we'll start with you."

Randy put the remaining cheese on a small plate and picked up the small cutting board. It was their regular paddle.

"No way!" Vicki protested, her face going pale as she looked at the paddle. "I'm not going to let you use that on me, especially for forty-five swats."

"Of course we wouldn't give you that many swats. You have to build up to it. This is just a little demonstration, a sample," Christie gently explained to her friend, even as Vicki was edging her way to the door. "We won't even make you take down your underwear."

"Why not?" Bill asked.

Randy and Christie exchanged a long glance, then finally Christie said, "Sure, why not?"

Before Vicki could reach the door, Bill and Christie cut her off. In a flash, they had her black tailored slacks down and had pulled her over to the dining table. With one of them holding each arm, they forced her to bend over and lie on the table. Randy stood behind her and used the paddle after he had lowered her lacy black underwear. He gave her twelve moderately hard swats with the paddle, six on each cheek. She screeched at each one, especially the ones that landed on her when her buttocks were tensed up. When it was over they let her up, and she stood there with her face red, glaring at them.

Christie took the paddle. "Your turn, Bill." She spoke with quiet authority and a degree of challenge in her voice. "Or did you think we were going to let you off after giving her a free sample?"

Bill looked at Randy and at Vicki. Vicki, her face red, was

rubbing her behind tenderly. She sounded angry as she challenged, "Are you chicken? Or is it okay for me but not you?"

Bill dropped his jeans and bent over the table in position. Christie pulled down his underwear and used the paddle. Just before she hit Bill the first time, Randy said one thing.

He said, "Bill, Christie's a lot harsher than I am. And of course, we went a lot easier on Vicki because she had a spanking first." He paused. "I have to warn you, Christie is probably going to hurt you."

As soon as he got the last word out, Christie started. As Randy had predicted, Christie was harsher than he had been with Vicki. She gave him a full dozen on each cheek, and she gave them to him as hard as she could. Randy and Vicki held Bill in placed but he did struggle and cry out. Christie felt a small victory that she was able to make him yell and squirm.

When Christie was finished, she silently handed the paddle to Vicki who gave him six more swats. The last six were not very hard, but Vicki enjoyed giving them to Bill. When she was finished, Bill stood up and pulled up his shorts and his jeans.

Randy said, "The whole point of this was to paddle Christie for losing the football bet. Now it's her turn and I think we've waited long enough. Zipper, love." He gave the familiar command to Christie.

She looked at the two spectators, then back at Randy. "Aw come on, they've seen butts before," he said.

She unzipped her pants without a word, and then laid down on the sofa on her stomach. Just like she always did, she lifted her hips letting him pull her pants down. Just like always, she pulled down her lacy underwear. He raised the paddle and brought it down hard and fast on Christie's buttocks. CRACK! CRACK! He gave her twenty-five on the right side, then he paused before turning his attention to her left cheek. He gave her the final twenty. The blows with the paddle were given faster and much more severely than the swats he had given her with his hand. They were much harder, more deliberately laid on. Each blow hurt more than the one before it, and the whole paddling was given ruthlessly right from the start.

Although the paddling made Christie's butt glow red and feel hot to the touch, she didn't make any outcry except faint moans. She squirmed quite a bit but she knew enough not to tense up her buttocks. She kept her cheeks relaxed throughout the whole paddling, even though it was given severely and hurt quite a bit.

"Boy! You really took that well, Christie," Bill said. "Can I?" At her nod, he patted her butt. It was warm to his touch.

"Well, we started it out slow and easy during baseball season and, you know, lower scores. Hockey hardly seems worth it," Christie explained.

"What about basketball?" Bill asked.

"The scores are too high!" Christie exclaimed at the same moment as Randy said, "Maybe next year."

"And back to how I learned how to take it well, we started without the paddle. Then we built up as I got used to it and began to trust Randy to know my limits. We bet for fun and a little excitement, not to inflict pain."

"I don't want to be rude," Randy said, "but don't you two have some place to go? I sure do hate to waste a glowing ass!"

Ignoring the other couple, he gave Christie a quick kiss on her bright red butt!

"Well, I can tell when we're not needed. I guess we better leave. Maybe we can go home now and find something to do," Bill said, patting Vicki on her fanny. "Something fun and sweaty and very, very sexy."

"Dream on, sadist." Vicki moved away from him, but she had a sly smile curving her lips. "You're going to pay for getting me into this."

"I didn't even hit you, all I did was help hold you in place," Bill protested his innocence.

"That was enough, more than enough." Vicki told him sternly, "You are in deep trouble now, mister."

"Make him pay, Vicki," Christie said, laughing. "For the pain and humiliation. I'm sure you can think of some interesting ways to do it."

"Oh, he'll pay all right." Vicki smiled as only a woman could, a wicked smile that made Bill fear for his safety.

"Good night. I'd walk you to the door but I'm busy," Randy hinted. "Don't let the door hit you in the butt on the way out."

And indeed, as soon as Vicki and Bill left, Randy put her ass and her whole body to good use. They made love right there on the sofa, fucking fast and furiously. They came to a tremendous climax and lay there for several minutes recovering before Randy took her to bed and made long, slow, tender love to her far into the night. Good night. Long night. No sleep!

My lover read this. I got a reward. His hand, tongue, belt and two paddles on my bare butt hard enough to sting (I pushed him a time or two) but not too hard (I eased him off a time or two). Can that guy give great rewards or what?

Two

Jesse: The Hard-Handed Janitor

Do you ever wonder about those anonymous men? You know the ones I mean, the janitors, deliverymen and window washers, all the men who serve us and keep us comfortable. Especially the ones with average looks. How far can one of these faceless men be pushed before he pushes back?

Jesse Guerrero, the building's head janitor, always came in late in the afternoon to straighten up the swank Law Offices of Eldrich and Tremain. He wasn't really there to clean, it was only an excuse to take a break and visit a friend. During the day, with the offices still busy and fully staffed, he only did light touch ups: Just wiping off tables and desks, emptying trash cans, re-shelving books and straightening the chairs in the law library, wiping off the table in the conference rooms, and sponging up the small kitchenette and the tables in the lunch room. Most of the staff hardly noticed him. He prided himself on being polite, quiet and unobtrusive while the staff was busy.

Later in the evening when the offices were deserted, except of course for the occasional late working law clerk, paralegal or junior partner, Jesse and his cleaning crew did all the major work. He and his crew polished the offices to a high luster. Every surface was completely cleaned. All the wood was polished, the counters sprayed and wiped completely clean. The desktops were carefully cleared, cleaned, and any papers and anything else was put back so that they were in the exact place they were before cleaning, although the office rule was that all sensitive papers were to be locked up every night.

Jesse noted if there was a clerk leaving things out he or she

25

should not, without reading the confidential papers. He reported to one of the firm's senior partners if he felt there was a problem, although he and his crew had all signed confidentiality agreements.

He knew the firm could be open to a major lawsuit if any information were to be leaked. After the desks were cleaned, all the floors were moped, vacuumed or scrubbed; he searched out dirt and grime until the offices were gleaming and perfect.

For about the last week, getting everything perfect had been easier said than done. There was a problem with a paralegal or young lawyer working in the law library late every night that week. She was beautiful and haughty, looking down on the cleaning crew as if they were insignificant bugs. She acted as if Jesse should feel honored to clean up her mess, and she really made a terrible mess. The law library was disorganized, with books and papers strewn all over, and wads of paper near the trash can but not in it. The small kitchenette had crumbs and spilled coffee covering almost every surface, even after he had cleaned it once that evening. The ladies room had to be cleaned twice. Even her desk was all cluttered, including several files marked "confidential" with papers peaking out of them. There were scraps of food in her office and the law library, and coffee spilled everywhere. Food and coffee both stained the carpet. Not only that, but in the smoke free building, there were cigarette butts and ashes everywhere. There was a cigarette burn on the side of an expansive coffee table. Jesse was livid.

"Ma'am, could you please try not to spill food on the carpet?" Jesse asked politely, controlling his temper. "And remember, it's against the law to smoke inside the building, not to mention disgusting."

"If you don't like cleaning up after people, why are you a janitor? Is it because you don't have enough brains to get a real job?" she snapped back at him, eyes flashing. "Maybe I'll complain to one of the senior partners about your attitude and get you fired."

"You want to complain about me? Go ahead," Jesse said in a

tight voice. "I've been cleaning these offices for six years. I think my record will stand up to your accusations. Bitch."

The sheer nerve of a janitor calling her a name left her speechless for a moment. He was long gone before she muttered under her breath, "Bastard!"

Jesse quickly opened a closet and took out a camera he knew was kept there for the use of the lawyers. He checked the flash, then quickly went back to where the girl was sitting and shot several quick pictures of the messy room, with her included in the pictures.

"What's that for?" she asked, jumping up from her desk.

"Evidence. You work in a law office, you must have heard of it. Just covering my behind, ma'am," he shot back. "What do you think I am? Stupid?"

"Give me that!" she ordered.

"Yeah, that'll work. Not! I'll let you have it in James' office tomorrow," Jesse told her, "and the three of us can discuss this. By the way, clean this office. I did it once, I'm not going to redo it because of you." He left the office the way it was.

Unbeknownst to the haughty beauty, Jesse had a secret. It was also a secret from most of the law firm's staff. Jesse was no ordinary janitor. He was the sole owner of the huge company that maintained a lion's share of the offices in the greater Los Angeles area. He cleaned this particular building himself for three reasons: First, to keep up with and train various crew members; new hires always worked with him at that building for the first ninety days. Second, it was his first building, the first building his firm had a contract to clean, which made it the start of his dream. And last, his very personal friendship with James, one of the senior partners at the firm.

If they knew about it, other members of the firm might wonder at the close friendship between the tall, handsome Yankee blue-blood lawyer and the shorter, stocky, round-faced Mexican-American janitor. The two men had little in common. The only outward similarity were the men's' smiles. They both had smiles filled with the secret to the joy of life. Less visible, they also shared a certain devilish outlook on life. Outsiders would not see these things so they might speculate as to why two such different men spent a few minutes everyday locked in James' office with a drink, whether it be coffee, cola, or even a cocktail, depending on their mood. Few understood the friendship, a friendship formed at a party held by *The Paddle Club*, a local and very discrete club for spanking enthusiasts, especially those who favor over the knee spankings.

The Paddle Club was an eclectic mix of all social strata and differing types of people. They had monthly parties in a beautiful old building just outside town. A discrete brass sign by the door read: PC Members Only. The club was a great place for fun and games, especially spanking games, but it was also a good place for socializing and many real friendships had been formed at the parties.

The club, even with its foundation in spanking, was actually very respectable. Drinking was limited, over-intoxication was discouraged and drugs banned completely. Spankings were often done out in the open, publicly, but always voluntarily on both sides. Code words were used to prevent things from going too far. The only time spankings appeared not to be voluntary and code words were rarely used was at a member's initiation, and then a club member acted as host and monitored things so nothing went too far. Nudity, to any degree, even just bare bottoms, was only by consent. Other than the spankings, all sex was private and normally only between married couples or life partners. Of course, no one under 21 was allowed.

Jesse and James' friendship had started at the club, at the very bottom. Literally at the bottom. The bottom of a young, blond woman that is. The two had met when Jesse was initiated but they had never really talked until they were both spanking the blond. Jesse was spanking her left cheek and James was spanking her right. At one point they looked up and as their eyes met, they exchanged quick grins and began an unspoken race to see who could paddle the now dark pink, curvy bottom the fastest and hardest. The race went undecided when the girl yelped and said,

"Stop!"

The blond jumped up rubbing her very red bottom, but she had a grin on her face and amusement in her eyes as she said, "You two are dangerous!" Laughing, she submitted to inspection to determine the contest winner. There was a drink riding on the outcome.

Jesse was determined to have lost. He bought drinks for James and himself and also for the blond victim. That was it. The contest was over but the friendship had just begun, and has grown ever since. Jesse had been over to James' for dinner many times and vice versa. James had since married, and Jesse had also become a friend with James' wife, Suzanne. Suzanne was a regal beauty who looked like a queen and had a bawdy sense of humor, and a real love of being spanked. She enjoyed light teasing spankings or even moderately heavy spankings. Sometimes she even enjoyed really hard spankings. She was open to all toys: Paddles, canes or a belt, but she preferred a hand, well applied to her firm, rounded, spectacular bottom.

At the club, Jesse had spanked and paddled Suzanne many times, and even on occasion been spanked by her. She could top with the best of them. All with James' approval. And now, three years later they sat in James' plush office, relaxing and talking over cups of coffee. Jesse showed James the pictures and told him about his concerns, especially his concerns about client confidentially. Then he got onto the subject of the mess.

"I tell you James," Jesse was saying, "that girl is something else. She's gorgeous with all the right curves, especially her tight little bottom; she's also bright, but as snotty as hell. She acts like it's a privilege for me to clean up after her, and she always, always, leaves a mess. Look at those pictures. She even threatened to have me fired if I didn't like cleaning up after her."

"You'll have to be more specific. We have several beautiful, snotty law clerks," James remarked with a grin. "I seem to have an affinity for hiring them. I can't think why."

"That's easy," Jesse smiled. "You just sit there in the interview and picture how much you'd like to take them over your knees and teach them a lesson or two. Bingo! They're hired. Have you ever spanked anyone in the office?"

"You're right of course, that's probably it. But no, I've never spanked any of them. The only woman who's been spanked in this office was Suze," James smiled as he recalled the event. "So describe this snotty brat a little better," he prompted.

"She's really gorgeous, about twenty-five, with shoulder length wavy blond hair, flashing blue eyes, great figure and a curvy bottom," Jesse smiled in remembrance.

"Janine." James sipped his coffee then leaned his head back thinking. "Yes, I can certainly understand her appeal, and I can also see where she could be taken down a peg or two. She can be a bitch. What's the big deal? You know better than most exactly what to do with a brat. Catch her working late one night and take her over your knees! Spank her until she sees the error of her ways."

"Some lawyer you are." Jesse was surprised because their spanking games were limited to willing participants. He expostulated, "That kind of advice could get me put in jail for assault!"

"With what evidence? What witnesses?" James asked quietly. "On her word alone? You know enough not to leave any marks."

"And who would she show them to anyway?" Jesse mused aloud, "Somehow I can't see Janine calling the police over and lifting her skirt to show them her red bottom. She'd be far too embarrassed."

"So there's nothing to prove it but her word against yours," James said softly." And I'd vouch for you."

"And there's also your extensive videotape cameras," Jesse responded to him, warming up the idea. "The ones you have for surveillance and to videotape evidence things in this office."

"The camera in this office, right here, focuses on the right arm of the chair you're sitting in, by the way. It's in a perfect position to catch the action if someone were getting a spanking over your lap." James commented, "But of course, you have absolutely nothing to worry about."

"So there will be no copies of the tape?" Jesse asked softly.

"Only the one copy, which Janine will not know about, the one which will find its way into my VCR at home where I will watch it with great enjoyment along with my wife," James smiled widely, "as she lays face down across my knees."

"Spousal abuse," Jesse teased, shaking his head. "Spanking your sweet wife."

"Only if I didn't put her over my knees once in a while. You know Suzanne." He smiled at the very thought of his beautiful, sexy, and kinky wife, and repeated, "You really know Suzanne, hell, you've spanked Suzanne on many occasions. She loves it."

Jesse, who'd had the beauteous Suzanne over his knees many times, smiled in remembrance and agreed.

Janine worked late that night. As usual she made a mess, leaving coffee rings on the conference table and tobacco ashes in a coffee cup, even though it was a non-smoking building. Crumpled paper was strewn everywhere except the trash can, and streaks of whiteout were on the telephone. Her desk, the small kitchen and the ladies room all showed similar signs of abuse.

Jesse was ready for her. He'd sent his crew down to another floor of the building and waited outside the law library. He walked in and caught her wadding up her notes and throwing them on the floor.

"That's it!" Jesse was adamant. "You lady, are a slob, a snob and a spoiled brat. You will come with me right now and I will give you a spanking!"

"I won't!" Janine's eyes flashed blue fire and her chin was high. Little did she know that she had never looked better. There was a trace of uncertainty in her tone, however. "You can't."

"You will cooperate with me or else I'll spank you on your bare bottom instead of over your skirt, and I will make sure it hurts much more," Jesse was firm, implacable. "And I can do it, believe me."

He took her arm firmly and led her down the hall without loosening his grip, then opened James' office and led her over to the chair. Still holding her arm, he sat down and pulled her over his knees.

"Stop struggling or its bare bottom time," he threatened harshly. "And remember, it will hurt more." He flipped a switch on the table near his elbow.

He began to spank her firmly but not too hard; she squirmed and yelled at him, cursing and kicking, reacting more from anger and indignation than pain. Gradually, the slaps came faster and harder. She kicked harder still and squirmed more, and continued to curse at him but he ignored her until she tried to put her hand over her bottom. He pulled her hand away and landed six sharp slaps right on the spot she was trying to protect. "No!"

Finally, he let her up.

"I'll have you arrested," she shouted, rubbing her behind. "Creep!"

"Call the cops," Jesse smiled. "By the time they come it won't even be red. Besides," he grinned, "do you want to explain this to a cop and show him your bare bottom? I'm sure he'd enjoy it."

"I'll sue then." Her voice was quieter, sounding less certain.

"Again, where's your proof?" he asked calmly.

"I'll tell my boss and get you fired." She was on her last threat and they both knew it.

"Do it. Tell your boss. Go ahead and get me fired," he challenged, and then taunted her by asking, "Do you think it's a thrill to clean up after someone like you. A nose in the air snob who's also a slob?"

"I'm not like that. I'm not that bad." She thrust out her chin combatively but sounded uncertain.

"No lady, you're worse." He stalked out of James' office leaving her behind without even so much as a backward glance.

The next day, Janine steamed and stewed all day. Finally, she gathered her nerve and went into James' office. She was both angry and shy as she told him how Jesse has spanked her.

"He threatened to do it again, but next time he threatened to spank my… " her voice trailed off.

"Your what, my dear?" James asked gently.

"My bare bottom." She practically whispered the words.

"But he didn't this time?" James hid his surprised expression.

"No," she said fervently, "he spanked me over my skirt."

James surprised her then. "Show me the um, evidence."

"There is none." She assured him, "It's faded now."

"Then go back to work, but hear this:" His voice got surprisingly firm and commanding. "I'm telling Jesse to use his discretion. If you ever treat him or his crew with disrespect or deliberately cause them any extra work, he will have my permission and my advice. He should pull your skirt up and your panties down and do the job right, on your bare bottom and very, very hard." He paused, holding her gaze with his and she began to shiver. "And if he does, I'll do it again myself the next day, with a cane. And I promise to leave plenty of evidence. Have I made myself painfully clear?"

"But sir!" James raised one eyebrow and she stopped, cutting herself off. "Yes sir."

"Go back to work, Janine," he said smiling. "I need a report of that deposition on my desk first thing in the morning."

That night working late again, Janine was nervous. She did not want another spanking and somehow she felt doomed. Most of all, she did not want that cretin of a janitor putting his hands on her, pulling down her... Unbidden, her mind formed the pictures: Jesse dragging her to a chair, pulling her over his knees, pulling her panties down and spanking her. Sitting there alone in the library, she flushed and shivered. She felt as if she were being watched, as indeed she was.

In the end, it was her nerves that caused her downfall. She made herself some soup and coffee, but she let the soup boil over in the microwave and burned the bottom of the coffeepot. She spilled coffee grounds on the floor, and then tried to wipe it up doing only a halfway job.

She took her coffee into the law library, against office rules, and spilled it on the computer keyboard and an expensive law book. She hadn't wiped off her soup mug after it boiled over so it marred the surface of the beautifully polished conference table. As she tried to wipe everything up with a wad of paper towels, she knocked over a bag of sunflower seeds she'd been snacking on.

Jesse walked in at that moment. He looked at the room, then at her, and shook his head slowly. Smiling, he crooked his finger, beckoning her. She got up from the chair slowly, tears already forming in her eyes.

"I'm sorry, I tried but... " She swallowed slowly, her voice freezing up, "I was so nervous."

"So you were anticipating my little visit." He spoke in such a friendly voice that she was almost lulled into a sense of security. Almost.

"I was scared," she admitted.

"And now you'll find out why." He ordered, "Take off your skirt."

"Please," she began.

"Now!" he said. "Or I'll add some corner time to your punishment."

"What's corner time?" she asked, curiosity outweighing her good sense.

"You'll find out soon enough." He ordered, "Don't make me tell you again. Take that skirt off now."

She obeyed, slowly sliding her skirt off. She stood holding it and feeling awkward.

"Leave it here on the table," he commanded.

She tossed the skirt on the table.

"Fold it!" He sounded exasperated.

Once again he led her into James' office. He sat in the chair and pulled her unceremoniously over his knees. He began to spank her sharply but not very harshly. She took the spanking with a good deal more restraint than she had the previous night. In fact, her first thought was one of relief. He hadn't pulled down her panties after all. That soon changed as the spanking got a bit harder and faster and started to sting. She squirmed, he stopped spanking her and pulled down her panties

"Now let's get started," he said with a smile as he settled in to give her a long stinging spanking, turning her bottom a bright red and making it very warm.

All her restraint fled as she began to kick and yell curses at him.

"Mind your tone and do not swear at me!" Jesse ordered harshly as he increased the strength of the blows yet again.

She attempted to cover her behind with her hands. He grabbed both of her hands in one of his and landed a series of blows guaranteed to make her bottom burn.

Finally, he stopped. "Now stand in the corner with your back to me." He commanded, "No, don't cover your beautiful bottom with your hands, I want to look at my handiwork. Keep your hands laced together at the back of your neck."

After a few moments he turned her around to face him. He took her hands in his and guided them down to cover her still warm behind. "Now how does that feel?" he asked her gently.

"It hurts!" she pouted.

"Good." He slowly moved in for a kiss. She made no effort to refuse him or evade the tender kiss. "It's supposed to. Now clean up this office and the mess in the library and the kitchen, and I'll let you have your panties and skirt back."

"Beast!" she muttered.

"Yes," he laughed, and kissed her gently again, lingering on her lips.

She cleaned the office, the kitchen and the law library, all the while naked from the waist down. Jesse watched, coached and occasionally swatted her bottom until everything was clean enough to gain his approval. Finally, he gave her a few smart swats and a quick, passionate kiss, then told her to get dressed and go home.

The next day she wanted to call in sick but she knew she would only be postponing the inevitable, so she gathered her courage and went to the office. When the rest of the staff broke for lunch, she was summoned to James' office. Jesse was there.

"I understand that even after our little talk you were a very bad girl last night," James said. "I promised you a caning. Take off your skirt and bend over my desk," he pointed. "Jesse will help you stay in position by holding your hands."

James walked across the room and opened a cabinet that Janine had never noticed before. He reached in and pulled out a thin, whippy cane. Jesse grabbed her hands, holding her firmly.

"James, not too severe," Jesse said. "She's really trying to improve."

"And we'll help her," James said evenly. He slashed the cane through the air making it whistle. "A dozen, Jesse?"

"No more than six, please," Jesse replied.

"Softy!" James chided.

"And not too severe," Jesse added, watching as Janine began to relax.

"Jesse, you're taking all the fun out of this," James moaned, winking at him.

"Not all the fun, just look at that nice, smooth pale creamy bottom," Jesse laughed. "It'll look perfect with a few red streaks. Of course, when I said six, I meant from each of us."

Janine squirmed against Jesse's firm hold.

"And now... " That was her only warning; James gave her six quick, smart cuts with the cane, not especially severe but each left a pink line.

The two men traded places and Jesse gave her six cuts, even harder, before they let her go. James put her into the corner and offered Jesse a cocktail. They sat and relaxed, watching her, and talking about her.

Finally, James said, "I'm going to lunch. Turn around girl."

She faced him and watched in dismay as he unloaded a tape from the VCR. He grinned, "I'll watch this tonight."

Jesse walked over to her and took her face in his hands. He kissed her tenderly and gathered her clothes, handing them to her.

"I'm sorry if I've been rude to you Jesse." She had tears in her eyes. "I really am."

"It's all right, honey." He kissed her again. "I liked your spirit and your attitude but I like your red bottom even more."

James came back from lunch and found his office empty. Jesse and Janine were both gone. James smiled to himself as he sat at his desk and called his wife. "My love, you'll never guess what happened today." He smiled as she spoke to her.

"Let me guess," Suzanne laughed. "You and Jesse are causing trouble again, right?"

"Of course," James said proudly.

"And there's a warm pink female bottom involved," she guessed.

"Right again," he sighed.

"And it's not mine, right?" She sounded put out.

"Only partially right," James teased. "Yours will be red soon enough, girl," he warned.

"Okay then. I love you," she said softly.

"Tell me later love, when I have you bare bottomed and over my knees," he ordered.

"I will but... " she sounded hesitant, "will it make you go easy on me?" There was a pleading tone in her voice.

"Hell no! You're getting it long and hard!" he almost shouted.

"Thank God! But what about the spanking?" she quipped.

"Do you feel like a severe spanking, Suze?" he asked.

"Truthfully?" She paused thinking, "Not at the moment, but I'll think about it all day and by the time you get home I'll be more than ready."

"So will I," he warned.

"Okey dokey." She hung up.

That night Janine made a mess again. It was not as bad as before; instead it was staged so that it would be much easier to clean up, but it looked messy.

Jesse came in, shook his head and grinned, "You know what's coming. Take off your skirt."

"Jesse, please don't," Janine said, but her pleading tone did not match the gleam in her eyes.

"Did you know, my dear, that the sofa in James' office folds out into a bed?"

"No, I did not," Janine said softly.

"It's perfect for resting after a spanking," Jesse said.

"Will I be resting alone?" Janine asked quietly.

"Not if you don't want to. You may want someone to kiss and cuddle you," he winked at her.

"I'm sure I will." Janine unzipped and dropped her skirt. "I'll bet I need to be cuddled for a long, long time."

At James' home, watching the tapes came first, right before Suzanne got a long hard spanking followed by a long hard cock. She enjoyed both very much indeed. As for Janine, she and Jesse had three kids before she ever got to see the darn tape, and then she had to watch it face down over his knees.

Does it help to find out that the faceless janitor is almost a millionaire? Or is it more important that he's slightly kinky? Anyway, you never know who you're ignoring and what he'll do to get your attention and respect.

Three

Personal: Command Performance

What happens when the teasing and kinky games get you hotter and hotter? How do you let your man know when the time is finally right to move on to a new game? A different, maybe even better game?

Ann always thought of Jerry as her lover even though they still had never really made love. Well, that's true but it's not entirely accurate. They had made love in several very explicit and sexual ways. They had just not had actual sexual intercourse. There was a reason for their continued abstinence of course, Jerry had a wife. He got married about three weeks before he met Ann, almost sixteen years ago.

After Jerry gave Ann that first memorable spanking, it was several days before they tried it again. Soon, they had a set of unspoken but firm rules. This is generally how they handled the sexual spankings: First, the person being spanked, and sometimes it was Jerry, was the one in control despite appearances to the contrary. That's what made it a fantasy.

Second, although the spanking could smart and sting quite a bit, the point of it was not to hurt the other person. It was for fun and done in a loving manner. These spankings were usually followed by the lovers using their hands or sometimes mouth to bring their partner to orgasm.

Jerry thought, and probably still does to this day, that these spankings were originally his idea. Being a man, of course he was wrong. He had been carefully led into the idea by Ann. The spankings were something she had wanted to try long before she ever knew Jerry, but she had never met a man she could trust enough with whom she could discuss the subject. That is, not before she met Jerry. She trusted him implicitly.

She had planted the idea of erotic spanking in his head almost without uttering a word. It was easy. He had always loved giving her a sharp, stinging swat on her firm well-rounded butt. All she had to do was respond to a swat with a smile or a casual remark.

"Ooh, that felt good," she'd say, rubbing the swatted area and grinning at him.

Or, "You beast!" She'd complain, "I'll get you for that." But her smile would be wide and wicked, full of promise.

Jerry was slow to take the hints, but Ann stepped up the campaign. She was reading when he came over one night, and she showed him the book. It was a spanking novel. She asked him if he thought it was sexy. On another occasion, she had an open copy of a book about people's sexual fantasies, with some of the fantasies marked with a faint red mark in the index. Jerry thumbed through the book and realized that all the marked fantasies involved spankings. She even used old John Wayne movies, the ones with spanking scenes, to plant the idea in his stubborn head.

Eventually the seed of an idea was planted. One night he told her that he wanted to give her a spanking. She pretended she was stunned, shocked and appalled. That was pure acting. What was real was the nervousness and fear she felt. She wanted the spanking but she was apprehensive about it too. Still, it was her first chance to test out her fantasy with a man she could really trust, so she allowed herself to be persuaded. Finally!

That first spanking was exciting but it was also too hard and painful. Much to Ann's surprise, it was a real spanking, not just a tease. She quickly realized that all the S & M books she had shown Jerry all involved serious and harsh punishments. A seemingly endless supply of English and German schoolgirls being severely beaten with birch rods and canes, many times until they were bleeding. While she enjoyed that first spanking thoroughly, what she really wanted most were just teasing, playful sexy spankings followed by Jerry teasing her and arousing her.

Finally she explained very clearly to him what she wanted. After the first time, the spankings usually took place with her rolling over onto her stomach on the sofa. Sometimes he would sit beside her and spank her firm butt with his hand, and sometimes she would lie across his knees on the sofa. He started using a warm up to get her ready for more spanking.

He always started with her jeans up giving her the first spanks right on the seat of her jeans, not very hard, but he always talked to her. He would tell her how long and hard he was going to spank her, promising to make her bottom red and very, very sore. He followed this by pulling down her jeans and spanking her over her panties. The teasing threats and chiding continued, the spanking got harder and faster, and he kept it up until she began to squirm.

After he had done that on several different occasions, when she was used to the spanking, things gradually changed. He began pulling down her pants and spanking her on her bare bottom. He spanked her with faster, more forceful spanks. It stung a lot more but at the same time it felt great.

Of course they found some interesting variations. For instance, one night when Jerry came over Ann was wearing her spandex crop top and shorts. They cuddled and snuggled on the sofa until she decided to provoke him. She lay on the sofa on her stomach, with her head on her arms and ignored him.

Immediately, he began to stroke her buttocks. Soon he tried to pull her shorts down. She refused to let him, so he spanked her playfully, right on her tight spandex pants. He rubbed his hand in gentle circles between the teasing slaps. Without a word, she rose and left the room. Soon she returned with a crystal bowl filled with warm water and a plastic bottle. She laid herself back on the sofa and let him pull down her shorts and the underwear that she seldom wore under them. Using a washcloth, he wet her butt and then squeezed a little of the floral body shampoo over the crest of each cheek.

He worked the luxurious shampoo into a lather covering her buttocks and then he began to spank her again, still very gently.

41

In between spanks he ran his soapy hands over her buttocks and into the crack between the two globes. He fingered her vagina, her clitoris and her anus. He began to spank her harder and harder, still using one hand to stroke and finger her. Soon after that things got very interesting indeed.

Another time while cleaning out a cabinet, she found a set of ping pong paddles and balls that she didn't even know she owned. She put them back into the cluttered cabinet. That night she asked him to help her clean out the cabinet and surprise, he found the ping pong paddles. He's a smart man; he immediately used one of them on her bare butt. It was wonderful! It was very loud and not at all painful.

They found another paddle the same way, (at least that's what he thought). It was really a small cutting board with a ceramic tile in the center. Ann saw it in a store, bought it, and that night she asked Jerry to help her with something in the kitchen. He found it. The cutting board paddle made less noise than the ping pong paddle, but it was more solid and hurt a lot more. A whole lot more. It never caused any bad bruises but it could really turn her bottom red and make it sting!

Except for the two paddles and one of Ann's old riding crops, they didn't have any of the usual S & M accouterments. No whips. No chains. No restraints. She told Jerry he could tie her up if he wanted to, but he refused.

Jerry explained to Ann that if he ever had her tied up and helpless he would not stop when she told him to, either when he was spanking her or fucking her. She retorted that if he ever fucked her without her permission, he could just dial 911 and hand her the phone on his way out the door. He wasn't sure he believed her, but he never put it to the test. It was a wise decision because she would have made that call.

As the playful spankings progressed, one thing they did do was to find a small, waist high table. They put it in her hallway. It was just the right height to bend over, putting her butt at just the right height and angle. The hallway had four doors, one on each end and one on each side. When the doors were all closed, the outside world was shut out completely. It was very dark without the light on, and the small hallway was even soundproof.

It was very rare for either one of them to wind up bending over the table in the hall. They wanted to keep it a fresh and exciting experience, not an everyday occurrence. They just wanted to know that the table was there, ready for them to use. And the paddles were right in the hall closet. And even several lengths of soft rope, if needed. Knowing that the room was there was spine tingling, exciting and dangerous.

One night he came in the door and handed her a little present, soft drinks and corn chips. He always brought something when he came over but it was usually nothing very expensive: a flower, a snack or a lottery ticket. It was just a small token. Money wasn't very important to either of them. Standing there in the foyer, he kissed and hugged her and rubbed his hands up and down on her butt. He spanked her right there, lifting up her skirt and reaching around her. She very seldom wore any underwear when she knew he was coming over.

He remarked, "I just love a woman with a round, firm butt." He gave her a smart slap. "And big, beautiful breasts don't hurt either."

She replied, rubbing her face against his shirt, "And I love a man with big, strong hands, a wicked sense of humor, and a well-defined set of muscles. But what the hell, two out of three ain't bad. Ouch!" He had slapped her butt extra hard.

He turned his attention to her three small dogs, greeting them. He had to since they were going nuts, jumping all over and biting each other to get his attention.

They went on into the living room and drank their sodas while they watched television. She had recorded the fifth game of the World Series for him. Jerry realized that it was a real sacrifice for her because Ann hated baseball.

It was not the first sporting event the couple had enjoyed together. She remembered a tennis match they had watched once and how Jerry kept slapping her ass in time with the player's strokes. When the baseball game was finally over, she asked him to spank her.

"Roll over," he said, always ready to oblige.

He sat beside her rubbing and even kissing her butt. Once, she felt his wet tongue slide up the crack in her butt. Shivers ran down her spine. She rested her face on her hands. He gave her a light spanking, only making it harder when she asked him to.

Occasionally when he hit her with an especially hard blow, he would suck in his breath and remark, "That one really stung, didn't it, baby?"

He only spanked one cheek, resulting in her butt turning pink on that side. Finally he stopped spanking her.

"Go get the ping pong paddle," he ordered.

She refused; she was enjoying the sensations of the cool air on her warm ass. He went to get it.

"You know I'm going to make you pay for disobeying me," he threatened as he got up to go find the paddle.

She was lying there relaxing with her eyes closed. She didn't know he was back with the paddle until she felt the rough texture of it resting on her smooth ass. He held it against the side he had neglected before. He began to rub it in small circles on her soft skin. Finally he raised the paddle and began to spank her with it, hitting the cheek he had neglected with his hand.

It was very loud. Not very painful, but very loud. She worried that the neighbors would hear the loud cracks of the paddle on her bottom. To this day, she doesn't know if they did or not. He spanked her with the paddle for a long time; finally he turned his attention back to the first cheek. Both sides of her butt became red and warm. Her cheeks stung.

He stopped and they had another soda and watched more TV. He sat on the floor beside the sofa and gently stroked her butt, savoring the heat of it. He gave her several deep, luscious kisses. It was wonderful.

He gave her another order, "Go get the heavy paddle."

Again she refused, acting lazy and very impertinent. Recognizing her rebellion for what it was, a desire to have him step up the force of the spanking a little bit, he brought back the paddle and used it with a lot more severity. She squirmed and pleaded with him to stop, but when he asked if she was going to be a good girl, she shook her head "no" and called him a jerk.

Apparently she hadn't had enough. When he was done they cuddled again, his hands teasing her buttocks and the moisture of her vagina. Finally he asked her for a favor. He wanted her to paddle him.

She told him to take the heavy paddle and go into the hall. "Get in there and bend over the table with your pants down. When I get around to it, after the movie, I'll be in there to beat you. And remember, I'm not as nice as you are. I'll beat you until your butt is black and blue."

In truth, she really *was* much more severe with him than he was with her. She hit him harder and faster than he expected. And she kept hitting him for a few more blows when he asked her to stop. He wasn't annoyed but he said he wanted vengeance. Ann was not a stupid woman. She sent him home. She wondered how he would explain the bruises on his butt to his wife. Oh well, he'd been telling her for years that they were getting divorced.

He turned at the door and said, "I'll figure out a way to pay you back for paddling me so hard. I'm a smart man." He kissed her.

"Did you say you were a smart man," she teased, "or that you have a smart-ass? I'll bet it really does smart."

He pulled her head towards him for another kiss. "Oh baby, you're really in trouble now."

"I'm shaking," she teased him.

Another thing she surprised him with was a movie. It took her a lot of hunting but she finally found a movie with two spanking scenes in it. There were no whips and chains, and not even any sex – just spanking. In the first scene the girl was spanked with a belt, and in the second another girl was spanked by hand.

It was the second scene that she showed to Jerry.

The girl was average and the man spanking her was older. It didn't seem very impressive at first. He started out spanking her on her skirt and finally lowered her skirt and panties to the floor. He never touched her sweater. Then things got very interesting indeed. The man was a master at spanking. His hands never stopped moving, either stroking or spanking the girl, and never too hard or too soft. He talked to her constantly as he rained slaps on her buttocks, thighs, calves and even the soles of her feet. At one point he pretended her rounded, red buttocks were bongo drums as he played a tune and sang along. When he finished, he had her sit on his lap and promise to be good, but not too good. He wanted to spank her again. And soon.

Ann had to play the movie softly with the sound turned way down because at the time, she had rented her spare bedroom out. After the movie, when Jerry wanted to spank Ann, they had to be quiet too. His hand was too loud, and so was a paddle. Jerry used his thumb to give her sharp little snaps with his fingers which hurt but were unsatisfying. Finally, he used a hairbrush on her. It was wonderful. Quiet but painful. Ann kept urging him on. At one point Jerry turned the brush over and used the bristles on her red, bruised ass. Then very gently he used the bristles on her moist pussy, and used the smooth handle inside her, playing with her until she came.

They didn't play any spanking games for the next few days, they just kissed and talked. They held each other and loved each other, without sex. That week Ann's tenant moved out. On Friday, Jerry called her from his job. It was an obscene phone call. At the end of the call he told her to be waiting for him, tied up and naked, bent over the table in the hall. It was payback time. He sounded very stern and cold as he promised her that this time he would hurt her, really hurt her.

He didn't expect her to really do it. How could she tie herself up? And why would she? She spent the time between coming home from her new job and his arrival figuring out just that. She was horny, aroused and excited by the prospect of waiting for him, naked and helpless.

She wasn't afraid. She could never be afraid of him. Jerry couldn't hurt a fly. She found the rope and used her experience with horses to figure out how to tie the knots. The secret was to make the final knot a slipknot, so that she could slide her hand into the knot and tighten it by pulling on it. If she wanted to, she could also pull the end of the rope and release the knot. She waited until she heard his car drive up, then she went into the hall and got into the knots.

She had placed the heavy paddle on the table beside her. She left the front door unlocked and turned all the lights in the house off, except for the foyer. The hall light was off, and she was waiting in the dark. A stray thought went through her head. She wondered what she would do if someone else showed up.

She heard him come in and greet the dogs. She called for him to come to her. It took a few minutes for him to get into the hall without letting the dogs in too. He was shocked when he turned on the light and saw her. She had waited just as he ordered her to with one exception; she was wearing bright red, lacy underwear! He slowly pulled down the lacy panties, inch by inch until they were down to her knees. Then he immediately began to spank her first with his hand; only on one buttock until that side of her butt was hot and bright pink, before he turned to the other cheek. Finally he picked up the paddle. He used the cool ceramic tile to rub her sore behind gently and slowly for several moments. He held the paddle still against her left cheek until she was in an agony of suspense. He brought the paddle crashing down on her left cheek with a loud crack and it began. For once, he hit her hard. Very hard. He was alternating the blows, going from cheek to cheek. When she couldn't stand it any more, she yelled for him to stop.

He stopped immediately, but only for about two minutes. Then for the first time in their relationship, he kept on spanking her. He hit her six more times on each cheek, still using the paddle, much harder than he had ever hit her before. It was her own fault. She had told him that one of her favorite fantasies was to be tied up and out of control, and have someone paddle her just past the point where she begged him to stop. He was finally fulfilling her fantasy, with a vengeance.

Ann had never liked to be whipped with a belt, and Jerry knew it. He took off his belt and whipped her with it. Six slashing cuts on her buttocks and six more across the tops of her legs. The belt left welts, another first in their relationship. It was severe, it stung, and it was great.

He untied and cuddled her for a long time. He didn't apologize for the harsh beating he had given her, or for using his belt. It was the first time in their game she had ever been hurt, really hurt. She guessed he could hurt a fly, after all. She enjoyed the experience, as painful as it was, but she didn't want it to happen again, not for a long, long time.

The next morning Jerry came over before work to check on her. He was feeling a little guilty and even shocked by what they had done the night before. Ann had to comfort him and convince him she was all right and that she wasn't mad. He was surprised to find out there were hardly any marks. She wasn't even in any pain. She was fine.

For the next month or so they didn't spank each other. Instead, they cuddled and watched movies on television. He pulled off her blouse and fondled her breasts. He even slid his hands under her skirt and used his fingers to bring her to orgasm. If she let him, he would use his mouth. She never lifted a finger to treat him to the same delights. She just laid back and let him arouse her. What he didn't know was that she was wrestling with a decision. Before long she had made up her mind.

She had started to write stories for him to read. Stories that amazed her when they came out of her subconscious. Stories that aroused him. One night when he came over, she told him to turn on her computer and read her new story. It was this story. He had to page down to read the ending. The ending read:

TURN OFF THE COMPUTER, IDIOT, I'M IN BED. GET IN HERE AND FUCK MY BRAINS OUT!

He did. He got into the bed and made gentle, passionate love to her with his hands, his mouth and his penis. He brought her to orgasm several times. At times he was thrusting so hard and fast that she had to put her hands over her head and push against the headboard, just to stay in place! Then he would slow down, and lazily slide his cock in and out of her cunt; so slow that she could feel every millimeter as he moved within her. Somehow he managed to roll her over so she was on top and give her a sharp slap on her butt. Then he would roll her again so that he was back on top.

When she wanted him to thrust harder, she used her heels to kick his butt. The same way she had always made her horses run faster. All the while he was whispering soft love words in her ear. It was the most magical and tender night of her life. He gave a performance worthy of a superstar. A command performance! Bravo!

Sometimes I just want him to hold me. Other times, I want him to make love to me. Lots of times I want him to give me a light, teasing spanking; at still other times, rarely, I want him to spank me as hard as I can stand it, to take me to my limits. Always, I want him.

Four

The Lash Resort Ranch

Some unusual training methods for young riders; all those riding crops are so multi-purpose, aren't they? And there's lots of rope for tying things (or people) up!

It started out as an old horse trainer's idea. He would take small groups of young adult riders, ones who placed in horse shows consistently but who never came in first or second, and make them into winners. His horse ranch was very remote, his clientele very exclusive, his services very expensive, and his methods? Very painful.

The riders and their horses had to live on the ranch while they were in training. The riders had to sign a written agreement that allowed him to use what he called "Limited physical punishment." What they were agreeing to was to let him beat them with their own riding crops, and worse.

The specialty of the ranch was a style of riding called gymkhana, which consists of timed events run around courses marked by barrels or poles. It was not as classic as English riding, with its jumping and dressage classes. It was not as rigid as Western Pleasure or Equitation classes. It was fast and furious, awards based solely on speed. One of the best-known gymkhana events is barrel racing, a common rodeo event sometimes reserved for women only. At regular horse shows however, men and women compete against each other, and barrel racing is only one of many events.

Because the event was timed and anyone could compete, gymkhana had a rough reputation and almost anyone thought they could compete and win, but the top riders had to be good horsemen. To win consistently a rider had to be athletic and fearless, and able to get the best out of his horse. A gymkhana rider had to contend with all out speed while maneuvering around sharp turns without going out of bounds, or knocking anything over.

The old trainer had a strict reputation, but it was mostly spoken of in whispers. It was rarely mentioned out loud. If he invited a rider to train at the ranch, he or she would have no definite knowledge of what was really in store for them, only vague suspicions. Suspicions that soon became harsh reality. He rarely offered to train anyone under 18 or over 21. That meant that although many of his young students were legally adults, most of them still lived with their parents. Somehow he found plenty of them: Parents who were only too glad to write large checks, and riders who reluctantly agreed to his rules of discipline.

His method was simple. He used the riding crops on the riders more often than the riders used the crops on their horses. The riders immediately got the crop for every error, at every practice session. Every time a rider ran an event at the ranch, that rider also ran the risk. The risk of having the crop land on his or her bare butt right out there in the open, with all the other students, male and female, watching. The resulting motivation to do a good run was strong. Really strong. Riding crops can sting like hell without doing any real damage. This method proved to be a strong incentive for the riders who were tired of winning sixth, fifth and occasionally some fourth place ribbons. They willingly, if somewhat grudgingly, agreed to put themselves into his hands to move up to winning first, second and the occasional third place ribbons.

It was a gold mine for the old guy. He didn't have to do anything for his ranch to turn a profit except train a few riders at a time. They did all their own horse care and the ranch chores. His wife, Dolly, loved the arrangement too. The students did all the housework. So if he had to bust a few butts once in a while, hey, life's hard.

His name was Jake Masters. He was a short man with salt and

pepper gray hair, a raspy voice, wiry build, bright blue eyes and a strong right arm. His wife, Dolly, was a cheerful woman, plump, with long brown hair just beginning to go gray.

This session the students were: Charlene, 18, with long, straight, brown hair always in a ponytail. She was slender with big, brown serious eyes. Tracy was also 18, but her brown hair was short and curly. She was curvy and bouncy, always smiling with blue eyes. Murphy, 19, had a sullen expression, long curly, brown hair and deep brown eyes. Rex, 20, had green eyes and short, sandy blond hair.

The first two days were run like a horse show, with three events being run in the morning and three in the afternoon, both days. For these two days only, no penalties were assessed; Jake made videotapes and notes of all performances, and wrote down the times run by all the riders.

On the third day Jake started out by explaining the rules. "Here's how it goes: We run two events each morning and two each afternoon. Every event will have a time limit set by me, and these time limits will get shorter as your training goes on. Any time you fail to have a clean ride within the time limit I've set for the day, you will ride over to me and I will give you advice on how to improve. Then without waiting for my order and without question or hesitation you will dismount. You'll hand me your riding crop, drop your jeans and underwear, turn around and bend over." He gave them a steely glance, eyes narrowed, but otherwise ignored the murmurs of protest. "After I've given you your beating, you will remount and run the course again. You have three tries to make a good ride in the time allowed before you have to go to the barn at the end of the session for what I call *further instruction*. I suggest you avoid that experience if possible. You will also get the crop for disobeying any order from either me or my wife Dolly. We'll start today easy, with single pole and a maximum time of 11 seconds flat. Any idiot should be able to run single pole in eleven seconds flat."

All four terrified riders managed to push and spur their horses around the simple course in the time allowed. That event was followed by barrel racing. This event had three barrels for the rider to run around in a cloverleaf pattern. It was run on a longer course in horse shows than in rodeos, and the times for top riders were high 17's and low 18's for a course set as long as Jake set his. Jake set a time allowed of 19.5 seconds. For the morning's events, Rex was the first to run. He went wide on the second and knocked over the barrel on the third. His time was 19.7 with a barrel down. He was scared to death as he rode over to Jake.

He got his lecture, which Jake ended by saying, "Well boy, I guess you're the first from this group to find out if it's as bad as they say."

He made a gesture, circling his forefinger in the air.

Rex blushed as it came home to him for the first time that he would have to drop his pants in front of the girls. Damn! He thought. I'll bet Tracy will never go out with me now, and I kinda liked her. He got into position with his back to Jake and the other riders, and dropped his pants. He bent over, bracing his hands on his knees, and waited. Jake beat him mercilessly, fourteen swats: ten for the barrel and four for the extra time. He pulled up his pants ignoring his fiery ass and remounted. As his sore butt came into contact with the saddle, his eyes widened but he didn't say a word. He ran the event again and this time his ride was okay.

Charlene was next; she had a good ride, and so did Tracy. Murphy's first ride was a disaster. He hit two barrels and was a half-second too long. Thirty swats. His second ride was also too slow, six more. He made it on the third try, much to everyone's relief.

"I'm sure disappointed, I only got to beat the boys this time," Jake grinned wickedly. "I'm sure we'll even things out for you girls this afternoon. Walk your horses for a half-hour, then brush them and put them up. We'll start our afternoon training session at two-thirty. You should have your morning chores done by eleven, then come up to the house and make yourselves some lunch. From twelve until two you're on your own. Saddle up and begin warming up the horses at two."

Rex found out during the lunch break that his beating had not hurt his chances with Tracy. In fact, by the end of the afternoon break the four teenagers had already formed into two couples. Rex and Tracy spent the break in the hayloft, kissing and making out. Charlene and Murphy took a long walk around the ranch holding hands. They found a few secluded spots to stop and cling to each other.

The afternoon training session was held in the large arena. The first event of the afternoon was called keyhole. It's an event that requires a great deal of precision from the horse and the rider. The course consists of a 20' chalk circle, with a 4' by 10' alley leading into it. The rider has to take off from the far end of the arena running full out as fast as his horse can go, enter the chalk circle through the alley, spin his horse around and run back to the starting area through the timing poles. Stepping over or on the chalk is instant disqualification. It's also very hard to avoid.

The riders had been warned. Their runs today must be clean and fast. Jake set a maximum time of 8.5 seconds. One rider rode at a time. The other riders, waiting for their turns, would help by walking hot horses to cool them down and replacing chalk lines as needed.

Charlene lined her big, bay gelding with the long narrow alley at the far end of the arena. She took a deep breath and tried to focus all her attention on making a good run and started her horse. She had the fast gelding in a full run. When she reached the circle, she sat down hard on him. She pulled him to a quick stop and tried to turn him around in a quick spin. Her stop was a split second too late and her horse had stepped on the back of the circle. She finished her ride with a time of 8.7.

She rode up to Jake, dismounted, and handed her riding crop to him. In spite of her fear, after she listened to the harsh remarks and detailed suggestions that Jake had for improving her performance, she unbuckled her belt and dropped her jeans. She turned her backside to Jake and pulled her underwear down off her butt, blushing furiously. She was shaking hard as she bent over, bracing her hands on her knees. Her imagination was running wild.

She was to get fourteen harsh swats with her crop. Ten were for being disqualified when her horse stepped on the line, and there were two for each tenth of a second over the limit that Jake had set. The swats hurt terribly and she had a hard time remaining in the required position for the harsh beating until, at Jake's suggestion, the boys came over and held her still. It had been even worse than her imagination. When it was over, she pulled up her pants and jeans and remounted gingerly, tears running down her pretty face.

"Again!" Jake gave the command. Her second try was a little better. She stepped out again but her time was faster, 8.3 seconds. It cost her ten more cutting swats. This time the boys held her in position from the start. She was embarrassed but grateful for their help. On her third try, she had a clean ride and a good time of 8.1. The whole group cheered for her, with Jake cheering the loudest of them all.

It was Murphy's turn next. His horse was a smaller brown mare. He made his first run and obliterated the keyhole; his time was 9 seconds flat. He got thirty hard swats. It was twice the usual penalty for hitting the keyhole because Jake said he had to have hit it at least twice to cause so much damage, plus an added ten for the extra time. He also got a long, unprintable commentary from Jake.

His second run was a little better. He still stepped out but his time was 8.6 seconds, earning twelve swats. His third try was a good time of 8.2, but he stepped out again. He got ten swats and the order they had all dreaded since the first day at the ranch. At the end of the afternoon's lesson he was ordered to report to the barn for some *further instruction*. He went pale at the news but made no protest. He was told to walk his and Charlene's horse around until his turn to ride again.

Tracy's chestnut turned wide and hit the side of the narrow alley leading into the keyhole. She had a time of 8.4. Although she tried to be brave, she had to be held in position by Murphy and Rex while she received her ten swats after hearing some valuable instruction. Her second run was a good ride with a time of 8.0. She was greeted with lots of cheers.

Rex was a timid rider in spite of all his macho cowboy swagger. He stayed in but had a time of 9.4 seconds. He got eighteen swats and a harsh promise. The promise that any time over 9 seconds in either of his next runs would require him to join Murphy in the barn for the special lesson later that afternoon. It was a stark, terrifying prospect. His second try, 8.6, was out. He got twelve swats and another threat.

On his third try he had a good ride and a good time of 8.5. He was shaking as Jake searched the hoof prints around the circle from his run. It was only a few seconds before Jake called the run a "clean ride." However it seemed like an hour to a visibly shaking Rex. He sighed a deep breath and accepted his cheers from the rest of the kids.

The students then set up another event, pole bending. This event consists of a row of 6 poles, 20' apart, with 2 timing poles. There are two versions of this event; in this version, the rider had to weave through the poles, turn and weave back. There were a total of 8 poles on the course, at a penalty of 5 swats for each of the poles knocked down. Jake set a time limit of 11.0. It was going to be a horrifying lesson.

Poles could be a strange event. It could be heaven if a horse was smooth, balanced and in control, just barely skimming the poles. It could be hell on a horse that was off stride, nervous or if he tried too hard to turn at each pole. The riders lined up at the end of the arena.

Charlene went first. She had a good ride with a time of 10.9. She took a deep, grateful breath, accepting the heartfelt congratulations from Jake and the kids. Then she began to walk her horse. Murphy was next. He also had a good ride and a good time of 10.8. Everyone cheered him. Thank God! He handed his reins to Charlene and went to work helping Jake. The work was easy; he leaned on a rake and waited until somebody knocked over a pole or the dirt got a deep rut from the horse's hooves. Then he reset the pole or raked the ground smooth again.

Tracy's horse got hyper and took off with her. She hit three poles and never managed to get the horse back through the timing poles. She was not a happy camper as she slowly lowered her jeans and underwear and received her punishment; again the guys held her in position. She got fifteen blows with the crop for the three poles down, and twenty more for being off course, thirty-five! Jake never gave anything but very severe hits. *"Never do anything unless you can do it right,"* was his motto.

She got back on her horse very carefully. Then she gathered up her courage, dried her tears and tried again. This time she kept her horse under control and used his speed to her advantage. She had a good ride with no poles down and a time of 10.2! Fantastic!

Rex gave another timid performance. On his first try, he knocked down a pole and had a time of 11.1 for eight swats. On his second try he had two poles down and was even slower than the first ride, 11.3, and sixteen swats. Jake warned him again; if he failed to do a good run in the required time with no poles down on his third try, he would join Murphy later in the barn. He took his third run with everyone cheering him on and he made it.

"Lucked out again, boy," Jake said. "But why are you so damn scared? You get more whippings this way than if you just went for broke. Much harder ones, too. I can't stand a jellyfish. What are you so damn 'fraid of? Falling?"

Rex looked stricken but he replied, "This is a new horse. I got him just before I came here. Just after you picked me, my old horse fell and broke his leg. I guess I am afraid, but it's not for myself. Really. I just don't want to lose another horse." By the end of this speech, there were tears forming in his eyes.

"Okay boy, I can understand that, no one likes to lose a horse. Think about this; in all the years of shows and riding, how many horses have you lost? Accidents happen and it's a terrible, terrible thing, especially if you love the horse. Thank God accidents like that are rare. Riders get hurt more often than horses. So ask yourself, do you still want to be a gymkhana rider?"

Rex nodded his head but he was still close to tears. "Thanks Jake, I'll try harder. I still have a problem though, I haven't had time to get to know this horse and I just don't have any feel for him yet."

Jake gave him a long look. "You will if you keep working. Group, all of you put some miles on those horses, go out on the trail and trot for two miles. When you're done, wash them off and walk them out for at least an hour. One of you take care of Murphy's horse for him. Murphy and I are going to go have a training session in the barn. He'll join you later." They all watched as Jake and a reluctant Murphy walked to the barn.

Charlene had a little extra concern in her eyes.

In the barn, Jake pointed to a saddle on a saddle rack about waist high and said, "Bare ass and over that saddle boy, and be quick. It ain't fair to let the others work your horse."

Murphy dropped his jeans and boxer shorts, and laid over the saddle. He wondered a little how this could be any worse than the whippings outside. He found out soon enough. First off, Jake tied him down with a lunge rope. It was made of flat, thin nylon and it was as harsh and uncomfortable, as it was humiliating. The thin edge could cause a rope burn if you were holding it the wrong way when a horse tried to pull away from you. It could also cause rope burns if you were tied up and tried to struggle, as Murphy soon found out. Jake picked up a heavy, wooden paddle with lots of holes drilled into it and began to paddle the boy's butt with very hard, slow blows. Each one landed with a loud SMACK. Each blow brought a loud yell from Murphy. Jake quit when he had given the boy two dozen. Murphy's butt was bruised in many places.

Jake told him, "I'm done with you, boy. Go out and take care of your horse, and I do mean get on him and ride."

He walked out of the barn, leaving Murphy to gather himself and get on his horse. The teenagers never knew it but Jake had something very important to do.

Shortly after that, Murphy joined the others. Silently, he took the reins and mounted his horse. He ached all over and sitting on a saddle was hell, but somehow he did it.

"What happened?" Charlene asked while the other two came over making sounds of sympathy. "Are you okay?"

She and Murphy were already a couple. So were Tracy and Rex.

"I'm sore as hell. That old fart made me bend over the saddle rack bare butt, and he tied me down! I hated being tied down, it was so scary and shit. He hit me a couple of dozen hard ones with that old, wooden, paddle in the barn!" Murphy told them. "You'd think I would be getting used to it, being beaten. You'd think we all would, but that was the worst thing I ever went through. I really hated being tied up."

"Is there anything I can do?" Charlene asked, concerned.

"Yeah, help me plan a way to get back at that old codger!" he said angrily.

"Let's not talk about it here. We'll talk tonight when everyone else is in bed," she whispered back.

"Good idea. The way I feel right now, that's all we'll do in bed," Murphy muttered.

She reached over and boldly slid her hand along his zipper. "Wanna bet?"

"Well, if I did manage to find a comfortable position to lay in, maybe on top of you, something might come up." He leaned over to kiss her.

"It's too bad we have to finish these horses," she laughed, "because something's up now!"

They finished caring for the horses, putting them up and feeding them. Then they had to go into the house. They had to cook dinner, clean up and do laundry, all under Dolly's strict eye. She was a friendly and cheerful woman but she could also be very demanding. If she reported any slackness or unfinished chores to Jake there would be a very painful outcome. Jake was not a dumb man. They paid him, yet they did all the chores. All he had to do was beat them black and blue.

Not that he enjoyed beating the kids; for him it was just another chore, a part of the job. He did it and he did it thoroughly and ruthlessly, but he didn't feel anything about it.

It was different with Dolly; she secretly liked watching the students get paddled, especially the male students. If she saw an especially good-looking young man get a beating like the one young Murphy had received, she would be horny from that point on until bedtime. Usually Jake found a way to bed her right after the beating, and she would be exceptionally aggressive; then she would still be excited that night. It was some of their best sex. It was also one of the reasons she could be so demanding, and it was why she was so quick to report to Jake about any wrongdoing by the students. Although the students didn't know it, she always saw the sessions in the barn. She got a signal from Jake and had a secret place from which to watch, a hidden vantage point.

After dinner they all gathered in the living room and watched films on the VCR. Not movies, but training films of past students, with the whippings included. They knew Jake videotaped their lessons, whippings and all, to use for future students. They were expected to have intelligent comments on every ride they watched.

At ten o'clock Jake sent them to bed. "And no foolin' around up there, hear?"

It was the only time Jake gave an order they could disobey, and disobey it they certainly did.

That night, for the first time, Charlene came to Murphy's room. She took care of him. She shared a cool shower with him and made him feel better. She knelt in front of him under the cool spray of water and took him into her mouth. She carefully spread her hands on his hips, carefully avoiding any contact with the purple bruises on his butt. She sucked him until he came into her mouth. They went to bed and made long, slow, gentle love well into the night. He forgot about his pain, and forgot about everything except being inside her.

Rex and Tracy were in the other bedroom. It was their first time together too. They made slow passionate love, taking turns with their hands and mouths, before her slid into her. They made love hard and long. Finally they collapsed into a deep sleep.

The students would have been amazed to know that downstairs in the master bedroom, Jake and Dolly were making love with as much passion and intensity as the kids had, and the old folks were even more inventive. After seeing Murphy paddled, Dolly wanted Jake to sodomize her. She knelt in front of Jake while he stood beside the bed and took him into her mouth for a short time, then knelt on the big bed and waited for him to ram his cock into her.

The next six weeks went on much the same with hard and harsh training sessions twice a day, followed by long and passionate lovemaking at night. The riders were improving, but the beatings didn't end. Every time an event was practiced, the time limit Jake set was lowered and the riders had to work harder to make a good run.

By the end of the six weeks, all of the students had undergone at least one session of extra instruction alone in the barn. Murphy had been in the barn at least three times. On one special occasion Rex and Charlene wound up tied side by side bent over the saddles on the racks. It happened when the keyhole time had gone from 8.5, to 8.0, and finally to 7.5. They both just plain failed to make good rides in the time allowed.

Jake placed two saddles on two racks, side by side, and gestured. "Two racks, folks! So there's no waiting!"

He tied both of them down tightly, and then made Rex wait while he paddled Charlene.

"Ladies first!" he said cheerfully.

He went to work. He put a lot of hard effort into beating Charlene's butt. Although he had set up his ranch as a school to avoid chores, Jake still believed in hard work. He certainly worked hard when it came to beating Charlene. Then it was Rex's turn and he put the same amount of effort and dedication into Rex's beating.

Neither one of the two, Charlene nor Rex, appreciated Jake's hard efforts one damn bit. They both yelled, squirmed and cried. When it was over, they both went out and took their horses back from Murphy and Tracy. They remounted to finish working their horses with tearstained faces.

Another time, Rex failed on two events in one day! He was given a session in the barn right after practice. A very hard session indeed, during which he was paddled especially severely. When it was finished, he was told to report for the second session at bedtime!

"I want to let your butt recover a little bit from this beating so that you don't get cheated out of the full effect of the second one," Jake told him.

Rex wanted to leave and quit the program on the spot but he had to admit that he was getting better every day. Was a trophy worth the pain? He quietly searched his soul for the answer during dinner.

At ten o'clock he was in the barn, bare butt and bent over, waiting. Jake was surprised to see him there; surprised and even pleased. He had expected the boy to turn tail and run, so he didn't let his approval show.

"Have you made up your mind, boy? Are you really a gymkhana rider?" he said in his usual gruff, matter of fact tone.

Rex turned his head and looked the old man square in the eyes. "Yes."

The paddle came down very hard on his butt. The session began. It turned out to be a much easier paddling than Rex expected. Except for the first six blows, it hardly hurt at all. He didn't even get tied up! Maybe Jake was human after all, Rex thought, and then Jake laid the last two blows on him. They were the hardest blows Jake had ever given him.

"*Human?*" Rex thought. "NOT!"

On their last Friday at the ranch they had a practice show with no set times. It was like a regular show; the fastest time with no obstacles down won. They ran six events. There was one exception; after each event there was a different kind of awards ceremony. The rider with the best time was declared the winner. The winner gave the second place rider two swats with the crop, bare butt, and hard. The first and second place riders gave the third place rider four swats. The top 3 riders gave the fourth place rider six. The group all ended up giving and getting lot of hard swats with their crops. They all ended up sore!

Jake told them, "You're off tomorrow. There are no training sessions. I will feed and care for the livestock. You can all take a trail ride. Get a picnic basket, your swimsuits and go up the trail to the lake and relax. Sunday, we're all going to the horse show at the county fair, and I expect you all to do good! I can't whip you while we're at the show grounds, so we'll settle up in the barn back here after the show. Then on Monday, you all leave and I get another group of butts to whip into shape."

They followed his instructions, more or less. They went skinny-dipping since each of the teenagers had forgotten to bring a swimsuit, accidentally. Sure.

After swimming, they had a lazy picnic and the two couples made love. Neither couple had any qualms about making love in the other couple's presence since they had all seen one another other bare-assed so many times. Although Jake had a rule against drinking at the ranch because the students were usually under 21, they found beer in the picnic basket.

"The old guy comes through like a human being once in a while doesn't he?" Rex commented. "Maybe it was Dolly."

They all dozed in the warm sun. Charlene and Murphy awoke first; they made love again, and then went for a swim. When Rex woke up he saw the other pair making love. It seemed like a good idea to him. He woke up Tracy and made love to her before joining the other two in the lake.

That night they were all eagerly looking forward to the show the next day. It would be their first real chance to find out how much they'd all improved. Rex was so excited that he talked to Tracy all night long and forgot to fuck her! Charlene and Murphy, on the other hand, made love to the point of exhaustion.

The show was a huge success. They had placed first through fourth in all 8 events. Jake kept frowning and writing in a note pad. The writing both worried and astounded them. What criticisms could he be writing? Was he really going to whip them back at the ranch?

Jake was actually scouting new students. He approached a girl of about 19 and explained that he was a gymkhana trainer. He told her about his ranch and prices, and pointed out his students. The only thing he said about the punishments was a comment that becoming a champion was a "long and painful process." He encouraged the girl to talk to his students.

She began to talk with Charlene. She was interested in finding out just how much she had improved under Jake's training. She asked Charlene about Jake's remark about the painful process.

Charlene blushed, "Let's just say that with Jake you get valuable pointers and instruction. Then you get a beating. You have the riding crop used more on your butt than on your horse's."

"You mean... "

Murphy interrupted, "She means that he beats you after every ride that doesn't come up to Jake's tough standards. He makes your drop your pants out there in the open, in front of God and the other students, and he uses that crop as hard as he can. You become a better rider one way or the other just to save your ass."

"Is it worth it?" she asked, shocked.

Rex joined the conversation. "It sure is. I've never done this well at a show," he grinned, "but don't tell the old coot I said that. He's mean as a rattlesnake already."

The conversation ended as the next event started.

When the highpoint awards were handed out, Murphy won, just two points ahead of Tracy. Rex was third, one point behind her, with Charlene one point behind Rex. She was thrilled to be fourth because, like all gymkhana riders, she was really competing against herself. She had been trying to beat her previous best times, and she did it in seven out of eight events! The whole group was flying high as they loaded up the horses and went back to the ranch.

The plan was to ambush Jake that last night and take turns giving him a taste of the paddle. They decided to wait and hear his notes. After all, he was a good trainer! Jake solemnly took out his note pad and told them that all he could write was compliments, and they certainly didn't need to hear them! All they needed to do was look at their awards.

The only thing he could think to do for them this last night was to give them a party. He set up a stereo with all the latest music playing at full blast, and volunteered to break out a bottle of cold champagne, maybe even two! There was even a table loaded with munchies and a large cake. It was decorated with the cartoon-style picture of a young man bent over a saddle, jeans down around his ankles, and his butt shaded red.

They looked at one another, holding a silent meeting. They agreed that it was better to drink champagne and celebrate than to ambush Jake. Jake and Dolly both drank and danced for a while before leaving the kids to their own devises. They had something to take care of, privately, in their bedroom.

Jake knew all along about the kid's plan for revenge. Every group planned for revenge, sooner or later. He would admit that they had good cause. The bottom line was: HE AIN'T BEEN WHIPPED YET!

I was a gymkhana rider, not a big winner but pretty good. Who knows how good I would have been if someone had been smart enough to realize the crop would work better on me than on my four-legged friend, Burgie. I used keyhole and poles because they were his favorite events. If I never see another horse, I will always be a horsewoman, if I sell all my tack, I will always keep my crop.

Five

Spanked By Email

Ok, this is purely a fantasy. I am far too cautious to go off and meet a man alone without knowing exactly who I'm meeting, and without letting someone know who I'm with. Most of the spankos I've met are the most decent people I know, but any group has its weirdoes. If you're going to let someone tie you up, please be careful!

The email was not posted through the group, it was posted privately, off list, and the email address the sender gave was unfamiliar to her. The unknown address did not alarm Terri since most of her emails came from the group and she rarely used individual email addresses. There were many people in the group whose email addresses she wouldn't know by sight. Many of her friends used made up names within the group. It was usually a matter of discretion. No one cared, it was left to personal taste.

However this message was a different story. It was brief, faintly stern, unsigned, and sent a chill up her spine. It read:

> *You deserve a punishment spanking and I intend to give you exactly that. It's been a long time coming and the wait is finally over. Come to the address below at precisely 8:00 PM tonight. Bring a heavy paddle, a thick leather strap, two wooden spoons, your flogger and a cane. Wear a short skirt with the tiniest thong panties you have.*
>
> *P.S. Bring some rope too.*

She took a long bath, soaking and gently playing with herself as she daydreamed about the evening ahead. Not that she was

66

definitely going, she'd been in the scene too long, and learned the dangers and precautions far too well of meeting with a stranger. She wouldn't go. Probably.

For some reason though, she was unafraid. That was odd because normally she was much too wary to meet a stranger in a strange place, especially a private home. If she did meet someone new, she met them in a public place and made sure a friend knew where she was. If possible she had a friend right there, in the restaurant, (or wherever they met) who could step in if there was any trouble. The worst that had ever happened was her friend got a free meal out of it.

It was just that she was sure this wasn't from a stranger. In her heart, she believed she knew who the message was from. There was a man in the group that she was attracted to. He was very handsome and a little bit stern. She knew he wanted her. He wanted more than just to spank her, she knew he wanted to be in a relationship with her. An exclusive relationship, both spanking and sexual. It had to be him.

She'd never been to his house and didn't know his address, but it was him, she was sure. Who else would write her such an email?

She wandered around her apartment, nude, letting the cool air wash over her curvy body, with its soft creamy colored skin still damp from the long bath. She had used her favorite bath oil and sprayed on a touch of her favorite fragrance.

Still not admitting to herself that she was going, she picked her dress and panties with great care. She made sure the dress set off her blue eyes and her wavy honey-colored hair to perfection. Of course, the dress also showed off her fairly generous curves. She left it lying out on the bed, ready to slip on. It wouldn't be needed though, she was not going. Not for sure.

Then she made sure the requested toys were neatly packed into a leather gym bag, which she left sitting by the door so she wouldn't forget them. If she went.

She dressed slowly, still protesting in her mind. Now she was not only going, she had decided to add to her punishment, to push the limits of her unknown chastiser. At 7:30 she dressed, did her hair, picked up her bag and got into her car.

She arrived at the address barely five minutes early. The devil inside made her sit in the car and wait until 5 minutes after 8 before she got out and walked up to the strange door.

It opened before she knocked. "You're late," he said.

Relief! It was someone she knew, a good friend from the group. Disappointment. It wasn't him, the man she thought it would be, but at least he was someone she felt at ease with. He was named Phil and he was a man she had played with for several months.

She sighed with relief; she felt safe and comfortable with him, but it wasn't the man she'd been dreaming about. Phil was a fairly short man, just her height, and was about 10 years older than she was. He had just a slight paunch, and brown hair that was thinning. His best features were his eyes; they were gorgeous, the color of dark amber, and filled with warmth and humor. He was polite, kind and surprisingly gentle. She liked him.

There was however, absolutely no spark of desire for him. Still, his email and what it implied, the fierceness, and implacability of the very real threat, intrigued her. It made her look at this gentle, almost timid man in a whole new light.

Knowing it was probably a very bad idea, she smiled gaily at him. She stepped into his house and he hugged her warmly.

"I'm sorry, I had tro… " she began.

"No excuses." He said without rancor, "You'll pay anyway."

He slid his hands down to her bottom and rubbed it gently before landing half a dozen quick swats on each side. "Unload your toys from your bag and lay them out neatly on the table, with your ropes next to them. Then come over here and stand in front of me. We have things to discuss."

She hesitated. "Now!" he snapped.

She did as requested and soon she was standing in front of him. "Why did you say I deserved a punishment spanking?"

"Why not?" he countered. "I don't need a reason, you're breathing and that's enough to get you into trouble. Besides, you're bratty, pushy, and you enjoy your spankings way too much. You even laugh. It's time you were taken down a peg or two. You need to have a bit of the fear and tension put back into your spankings."

"What are you going to do?" she asked softly.

"Everything!" he grinned at her. "We're alone. No safe words, no other people and no mercy. You're going to get a real spanking. Are you scared?"

"A little, but I trust you," she answered with total honesty.

"And so you should trust me, a little," he said flatly but his eyes were gleaming. "We'll start with a little hand spanking for a warm up. Lay yourself across my knees."

At the words "warm up" she relaxed a bit; in a real punishment spanking there was no warm up, nothing to ease into the spanking or dull the pain. She did as requested and he raised her skirt then gently stroked and fondled her warm, round bottom. He tickled and played and explored her before he began to spank her very gently.

"I notice you didn't follow my instructions," he said sternly. "I told you to wear your skimpiest thong. These panties are very nice but I know you have some very sexy, tiny things."

"I'm sorry," she said softly.

"Don't worry, my dear," he laughed. "You'll pay for not obeying me, and pay very well for it."

He continued the gentle spanking. She was almost disappointed because she had built this up to a much harder spanking in her mind and she was ready for it. The feeling was brief. The spanking built up quickly, both in speed and in severity. Far too quickly to be a decent warm up.

Soon she began to squirm and wiggle in protest, little yelps coming every time a particularly good swat landed.

"It's time for us to get started, my dear," he said happily as he pulled her panties down. "About a hundred good ones with my hand, maybe two, and then we'll go on from there. Of course, there's still the matter of your tardiness. Say, fifty extra with the hand for that, well laid on of course. We'll take care of the panties vs. thong issue with one of the toys. And my dear, any further disobedience will not be dealt with by hand. Count for me."

The spanking started. It was hard but not overly harsh, she'd felt worse, and knew she would feel worse again before the night ended. She counted every spank. The first fifty were fast and loud, and her bottom was warm and throbbing by the time he finished them. The next fifty were harder and faster, and she squirmed and yelled at him. He ignored her protests until finally…

"You bastard!" she yelled.

"You'll pay for that insolence when we move up to the wooden spoons," he said coldly. "And believe me, you'll pay dearly."

"I'm sorry!" she protested.

"Not yet, you're not," he replied, still spanking her. "But you will be."

The final fifty were harder and faster still and she had quite a time counting them. The spanks came faster than her words. She also had a real struggle not to cuss him out again. Thankfully, she managed. He did not stop there however, he let go with a final barrage of harsh spanks that made her bottom jiggle and had her behind on fire. Finally he stopped.

He let her stand in front of him and he gently removed her skirt. Her bottom was already very red and blotchy.

He told her to go into his bedroom. He put on the radio, which was tuned to a Latin music station. He got on the bed, sat up against the headboard, and told her to lie across his lap. He used the two wooden spoons as if they were bongos to keep rhythm with the music, drumming on her bottom with abandon and total enjoyment. It hurt but it was not overly severe. It was a brief and fun respite, right up to the point where he got serious and punished her for calling him a bastard.

After a couple of songs, he put the spoons away and unpacked the paddle. The respite was over. He paddled her with loud, harsh smacks. They were spaced out with a good second or so between every smack. Each one was hard. Each made her squirm and wiggle. He paddled her for a long, long time.

"Now we get to the matter of following orders," he said, "Remember the thong?"

He swung the paddle quite a bit harder, another twenty-five smacks. "Will you wear the clothes I tell you to next time?"

"Yes," she said softly. "Probably."

He raised the paddle.

"I will!" she quickly shouted. "I promise!"

"Good girl." He stroked and petted her sore bottom tenderly for a long time; she relaxed and reveled in the feeling. His clever fingers even slipped into an area they had never touched before. Just as she thought about protesting, he stopped.

"Go get your leather strap," he ordered.

She scrambled off the bed and walked into the living room to get her strap. It was not a very severe strap but it had a nice sting, and she usually enjoyed the feeling. This time he stood beside the bed and swung the strap not particularly hard but covering her entire bottom, and going down onto her thighs. She hated having her thighs spanked and he knew it. He focused on her bottom but enough blows landed on her thighs for her to know it was deliberate.

He left her there this time and walked into the living room himself, coming back with her deerskin flogger and a few other things in his hands. He also had the cane and the rope.

He began to flog her. The flogger was very soft, and even though he swung it smartly, there was very little pain from it. It was more of a thud that felt stimulating and, well arousing, with just a touch of a sting. Like the wooden spoons, she enjoyed this part of her punishment. She laid there and relaxed, feeling cherished and cared for. It was hard to explain but a good spanking always made her feel cherished.

Suddenly he stopped. "You're enjoying this far too much," he said sternly. "Stand up."

She stood where he told her to at the end of the bed, and tied her to the bed frame. Now she was nervous. She hated the cane, and he knew it.

He picked up the cane and whistled it through the air several times, causing her to give a little shiver of anticipation before he slashed her behind with it. He gave her a full dozen cane strokes, good hard ones, but not excessively severe before untying her.

He ordered her to stand in the corner. Picking up all her implements, he carried them into the living room. He got something from the kitchen and returned to the bedroom.

In the softest tone he'd used with her all night, he asked her to come over and lie down on the bed. She did it, settling in, with her head cradled on her arms and her arms resting on his pillow. She was more relaxed and at peace than she'd been in a long time. Her bottom stung, but not outrageously.

He began to tease her, tickling and pinching her round bottom. He even gave her a nip, right on a rosy crest. In the small bowl he'd brought from the kitchen, he had some ice cubes which he ran gently over her hot bottom. He stroked and tickled her.

His clever fingers even crept back into what she thought of as the forbidden zone, the crevice between her bottom cheeks. His unerring fingers found her moist clit, and he used them, bringing her to a shuttering orgasm. Then he smoothed soothing lotion all over her tender bottom.

He stood by the bed, pausing only to look into her eyes. She nodded, without a word and he quickly striped off his clothes and got into bed with her.

He wasn't the man she'd been fantasying about, true, but after that night she began to fantasize about Phil. He may not look like a dream man but when he got going – WOW! He *really* got going.

In the spanking scene, even the mildest looking man can have a hidden side. Also it's funny, but looks don't seem as important to spankos as to vanilla folks. Even the ugliest girls are spanked well and often, and even the nerdiest men can be terrific tops. And isn't that nice?

Again though I caution all of you, men and women, to know who you're going to meet, and to meet in a public place if you can. Also, it's a very good idea to let a friend know where you are and who you're with. I've never had a bad experience in the scene, but I have heard of some.

Six

A Painful Lesson

Reading, writing and 'rithmeti, taught to the tune of a hickory stick – by a flat out foxy hunk of a teacher!!! Would a girl be bad just to get his attention? Would she like the attention she got? I want to say up front, I don't approve of student/teacher relationships at all, but it was still fun to write.

"Shelly Maxwell, stop talking in class and pay attention, and I mean this instant!" Mr. Johnson said sternly. "If you don't, you will stay after class! Do you remember what I said would happen the last time I kept you after class?"

Shelly, a slender girl, glared at her teacher. She felt as if she was still in high school even though she had graduated, turned nineteen, and was now in the community college. She had long, straight brown hair and large brown, defiant eyes. She was the class clown and was too caught up in playing around for the boys in the class to listen to a mere teacher. Even Mr. Johnson. She never listened to what Mr. Johnson told her, so she certainly had no idea what he had said. She looked at him of course; for a teacher he was really hot, but listen? No way, José. She was only enrolled in the college because her father had given her a choice: go to college or get a job!

She would be done with this class in about a month, with luck, and Mr. Johnson was only a community college teacher and a substitute anyway. He was teaching her English Lit class until the end of the year because old Mrs. Simpson had broken her left hip in an auto accident. He was as boring as Mrs. Simpson, but the scenery was sure a lot better!

As Mr. Johnson started to turn back to the blackboard, she shot him the finger. Unluckily for Shelly, Mr. Johnson had the great peripheral vision that so many teachers are blessed with. He saw her defiant gesture out of the corner of his eye. However it was certainly not the worst thing Shelly had ever done in class or at school. It was not even close to it.

About a month earlier Shelly had been caught drinking on campus. A few days before that, Mr. Johnson had caught her cheating on a quiz. Shooting him the finger a was a minor infraction, no big deal, except for one thing: for Mr. Johnson it was the last straw. At the end of the hour, the usually cheerful Mr. Johnson sternly told her to stay after class.

Shelly was annoyed, but not really alarmed. It was not the first time Mr. Johnson had kept her after class. He had done it twice before, each time Shelly had tuned him out, not even bothering to listen to his urgent lectures and stern threats. She acted as if she was still a child in high school, never recognizing that she was behaving like just that, a child, and a spoiled brat at that.

Who needed him anyway? He was just a substitute English Lit teacher. If he wasn't such a hunk with his sexy blue eyes, she wouldn't even bother to show up for class every day. It was worth the boredom of English Lit class just to look at him. She vaguely wondered what it would be like to kiss him as she settled into her chair and waited for the lecture to begin.

When the rest of the students were gone, Mr. Johnson didn't begin to lecture her. Instead, he walked over to the door of the schoolroom and turned the lock with a loud click. He pulled down the window shade on the door. Nervously, Shelly wondered what he had in mind. He wouldn't try to molest her, would he? Shelly felt a shiver run through her at the thought. It was a shiver of budding excitement, not fear.

"Do you remember what I told you last time, about what would happen if I ever had to keep you after class again?" he quietly repeated the question he had asked earlier.

Shelly squirmed in her seat, suddenly uncomfortable, trying to remember. She hadn't listened to a word he said, but some bits and pieces seemed to echo in a remote corner of her mind.

Finally one word came clearly into focus: Spanking. Her big brown eyes widened in shock as she remembered: Mr. Johnson had actually threatened to give her a spanking!

Watching her, Mr. Johnson could tell the exact moment when the girl remembered his threat. He saw the fear and disbelief come into her expressive brown eyes. She was defiant, but he was deadly serious. He fully intended to carry out that threat, right there in his classroom.

Even if it cost him his job, it would still be worth it; at least he wouldn't have to put up with any more annoying adolescent brats. Hell, the way he was feeling at that particular moment, he didn't care if he wound up in jail. He was tired of their teenaged insolence, their swearing, their smoking, drinking and drugs, and most of all their know-it-all attitudes about everything, especially about sex.

He felt as if he would go totally insane if he heard one more childish, spoiled, eighteen year old tell him, "You can't do anything to me, I'm over eighteen and I'm an adult!"

Now, finally, he was going to get a little bit of revenge. That Shelly was the prettiest girl in his class didn't have a damn thing to do with it!

"I'm going to spank you like the immature little brat you are! Lay across my lap," he ordered as he sat at his chair and began to roll up the long sleeves of his crisp white shirt. "Right now!"

"But Mr. Johnson," she protested, "you can't spank me! Spanking is not permitted at this school; it's not even permitted in this state. I'll tell my parents and get you fired."

As she said this, he grabbed her arm and dragged her to the chair, ignoring her protests and her struggles to get free.

"So what? You'll already have been spanked. I'll just have to tell your parents why I spanked you and I can make you sound like you were even worse than you really were. I can bring up incidents of drinking, cheating and who knows what else? I know we reported some of these things to your parents; why haven't they done something about it themselves? Also, you might consider it embarrassing to have everyone know that you got a spanking like a spoiled little girl," he answered. "Besides, I'm only a substitute anyway; I can always get another job, probably even a better job. Stop resisting and submit or I'll add more to your punishment."

Shelly stopped struggling because she knew why her parents hadn't punished her after they got the reports from the school. Her mother had kept them hidden from her father. If her Dad had found out he would have probably punished her severely. Even with her mother protecting her, her father was getting frustrated by her behavior lately. In fact, he had recently been threatening to spank her himself; spank her very hard like he had when she was a little girl.

The very idea outraged Shelly. Her Dad was nuts! He didn't seem to realize that at nineteen, she was already a grownup. He probably would have done it already but her mother, a big, bossy woman, had stopped him. He was more likely to praise Mr. Johnson than to protest to the head of the community college district.

"This probably won't hurt very much," she thought. "He can't possibly spank me as hard as my Dad used to. It might even be kind of sexy because after all, Mr. Johnson is such a fox. Maybe he'll get turned on by my naked bottom and forget about spanking me altogether!"

Slowly, with a little trepidation and great deal of hesitation, she laid herself over Mr. Johnson's lap. She braced her hands on the floor, with her buttocks straight up in the air. Her long brown hair was dragging on the floor.

He struggled to raise her tight skirt, exposing her pale round ass only partially covered by lacy blue panties. He swallowed hard at the sight, trying to remember that he was supposedly punishing her, not molesting her. After gently feeling her bottom, an action he just couldn't resist, he began to spank her with hard, slow blows. CRACK! CRACK! He concentrated on her left cheek, landing over and over on the same small spot. He pulled down her panties just enough to check; sure enough, the area was turning a bright red and it felt hot.

She began to squeal and protest, "OUCH! OH MY GOD! STOP!" Mr. Johnson kept raining hard slaps on the area, making it a darker and darker red but not bruising her.

Finally, he turned his attention to her right cheek and began to give it the same relentless treatment. Shelly cried and yelled. She tried to keep quiet so no one would hear her shame, but Mr. Johnson made it impossible. Ruefully, she admitted to herself that he could indeed spank as hard as her Dad could.

At last Mr. Johnson stopped spanking her, but he realized he still hadn't been severe enough to make a permanent impression on her. She had managed to keep her attitude of defiance.

"Go and get your hairbrush out of your purse!" he ordered.

By now, Shelly had learned not to argue or protest. She obeyed instantly, walking awkwardly over to get her brush; her bottom was on fire and her legs were made weak with fear.

"Take down your underpants and lay down again across my lap," he ordered. His order had brought her to a new level of fear. She reached up under her tight, black skirt and reluctantly pulled down her powder blue nylon underwear. Obeying his gesture, she placed herself gingerly in position back over his lap with her panties down around her knees. She couldn't help feeling the hardness of him up against her belly. It should have been arousing but it wasn't. She was shaking badly.

Immediately, he began to beat her with the back of the brush, reinforcing the pain of the previous spanking. The brush was made of wood and each blow seemed to sink deeper into her bottom, all the way down to the muscles. Shelly squirmed and yelled as her bottom became redder still. The spanking continued in spite of her protests. After a while, he turned the brush over and harshly spanked her with the stiff bristle side down. The agony was excruciating. Little blood blisters began to form on her buttocks. She could no longer stop herself from screaming.

It only took a short period of time, time that seemed like forever to Shelly, before he finally stopped spanking her. She was too hurt to move and so she just lay quietly on his lap until he told her sternly to get up.

He ordered her to stand with her back to him and hold her skirt up so that he could admire his handiwork. She felt thoroughly embarrassed and humiliated, standing there with Mr. Johnson looking at her bare, red butt. She was crying openly; her eyes were red and her face was wet from her tears. She was in a great deal of pain as her butt felt swollen and hot, and it throbbed terribly. At last, he told her to pull up her panties and go home.

As soon as she stepped into the hall, she realized that some of the teachers, the ones who had been working late, were standing outside the classroom door. There was even a scattering of students. Witnesses, Shelly thought, they had heard everything. Then she realized that they had thoroughly enjoyed the pleas and screams they heard coming from the room. She realized they would not help her; if they were ever questioned they would be blind and deaf.

"Troublemaking little flirt deserved every second of it," she heard one teacher say.

"I wish it had been me," another replied. "I think it was long overdue."

A few of the teachers even applauded. That, almost as much as the terrible spanking itself, brought home to Shelly how much harm she had done in her teachers' eyes. She resolved to change her ways. Besides, after that day, it wasn't the boys in the class she wanted to flirt with, it was Mr. Johnson.

After the painful spanking Shelly worked hard to improve her behavior, and she had succeeded to a small degree. She softened her appearance by toning down her makeup and dressing better. She improved her attendance and was quieter, if not attentive in her classes. She also turned in some of her assignments. In most of her classes she had even improved her grades. Her grades in English Lit however were lower than ever. She spent so much time staring at Mr. Johnson in class and having explicit daydreams about him that she almost never heard a word he said.

She lay in bed at night thinking of Mr. Johnson with her hand gently working between her legs. She remembered everything about him: his handsome chiseled face, curly brown hair, bright blue eyes and great buns. She loved watching his buns as he wrote on the chalkboard. She imagined his voice saying romantic and erotic things to her. She ran her hands gently over her own ass as she remembered the feeling of him while he gently stroked her butt before he spanked it, and she even remembered the feeling of the severe spanking itself. The fear, pain and absolute, total helplessness. Her fingers worked furiously at the small spot between her legs and she moaned softly as she combined her memories and her fantasies.

The other students in her school would be shocked; not at her fantasies, but at who they were about. A teacher. They would be even more shocked if they ever found out the truth: In spite of her wild reputation at school, Shelly was a virgin. Almost everyone knew Shelly would do it with any guy but no one could actually say which guys she had done it with. The boys she had dated all bragged about having her and none of them would ever admit the truth.

Whenever she went out with one of them, she usually wound up wishing that she had stayed home because the guy would be so busy trying to get her to live up to her reputation that she never had any fun. Most of her dates never wanted to go anywhere or do anything but have sex, and Shelly was just smart enough to realize that some of them didn't really care for her at all.

She spent her nights alone, dreaming of Mr. Johnson and plotting to get him. She was no longer interested in the boys in her class, she wanted a man. A real man. She wanted Mr. Johnson. It cost her another, even more painful spanking, but before his assignment as a substitute in her class was over, she got him.

It happened during the last week of class, when the class was taking a final exam that would count for one-third towards their final grades. Mr. Johnson caught Shelly cheating off Karen's paper. He gathered up the two papers and compared them. Karen's paper was completely finished but Shelly's still had a few answers missing. Except for that, the two test papers were identical.

After he questioned Karen and satisfied himself that the slender blond girl with scared green eyes was unaware that Shelly had been copying off her paper, he sent her home. Shelly was in a panic! She had cheated because she didn't want Mr. Johnson to know that she wasn't listening in class. She didn't want him to realize that the whole time she sat in class staring so intently at him, she was indulging in the most erotic daydreams her young mind could come up with.

Shelly could remember all too well the pain she had felt when she was the recipient of Mr. Johnson's anger, especially when he took that anger out on her buttocks. The last time she hadn't been able to sit down comfortably all weekend.

"You don't learn, do you? I'll just have to punish you again, much harder than before. This time it's really going to hurt!" he threatened.

"No!" she shrieked in panic and fear. "Not again! This time I *will* report it, I swear I will. I was hurt too much last time!" She started to back out of the room. "I'm going home! You can't stop me!"

"You may not have liked it last time, but it did turn you on, and you know it! You stopped flirting with the boys in the class and started to flirt with me! Did you think I wouldn't notice?" He grabbed her by the hand, ignoring the sudden shock in her face. "However you are right about one thing, you are going home! I'm going to spank you so hard that I would never get away with it. At least not without your parents finding out about it, so I'll get their permission and do it right in front of their faces!"

Mr. Johnson completely ignored her tears and pleading as he more or less dragged her to his car, an old red Ford Mustang, and shoved her into it. He drove to her home and then more or less dragged her out of the Mustang and into the modest, slightly run-down house.

Her mother was horrified to have her daughter dragged home by a teacher, to say the least. She argued fervently in favor of leniency, but at Mr. Johnson's determined request she called her husband at his office and told him to come straight home. Shelly was ordered to wait in her bedroom upstairs. She lay on her bed in the small room with the walls full of rock star posters, and stared off into space without really seeing her surroundings.

Shelly's mother tried to make Mr. Johnson as comfortable as possible in the living room as she continued to argue with him. She had him sit on the drab beige sofa and served him a large glass of freshly squeezed orange juice. She repeatedly tried to persuade him not to punish her daughter. She even begged and pleaded with him not to flunk Shelly for cheating on the final exam. She wanted him to just forget the whole incident. Now, Mr. Johnson thought, I know why the girl was so much damn trouble.

Shelly's father finally came home. He was a slight little man, beginning to go bald. He was not shocked to find out that a teacher had brought Shelly home. He knew the girl was trouble but he was henpecked by his wife and couldn't bring himself to face the bitching he knew would have to face if he did what he wanted and disciplined the girl. This time though, he'd had enough. Finally Henry put his foot down and agreed to Mr. Johnson's request that he be allowed to punish Shelly.

"In fact," Henry stated, looking sternly at his wife, "when you get through with her, I'm going to add my two cents worth, right on her behind!"

"Henry!" exclaimed Shelly's mother. "You cannot both beat the poor girl! I simply won't allow you to do it. It's too barbaric!"

"Martha! Shut up!" Henry bellowed, a trace of an old British accent entering into his speech. "You're not too old to have hot red bottom cheeks yourself, dearie. Do ya get my drift, love? I've allowed you to henpeck me long enough. One more word and you get it too."

"But Henry!" she shrieked.

"That's two! That does it, Shelly gets it first and you second! Now sit down and be quiet. Mr. Johnson, you will do me the courtesy of lending me a hand with both of them, won't you?" Henry asked politely.

"Indeed I will, with pleasure." In a whisper he said to Henry, "Sounds like fun!"

Martha was so shocked that for once she was very quiet and subdued as the two men went up to get Shelly out of her room. She really didn't believe Henry had it in him, but she wasn't sure. Up in her room Shelly was ordered to take off her skirt and panties and walk downstairs without them. She was told to take off Mr. Johnson's belt and roll up his shirtsleeves. She was then instructed to bend over and hold on to the seat of a chair with both hands. She was told she would get eighteen lashes with the belt and was warned that if she moved her hands off of the seat of the chair, the punishment would have to be started again from the first lash.

Mr. Johnson started off by spanking her with his hand. Then he whipped her mercilessly with his belt, leaving long, red welts with every blow. The beating took less time than the punishment in the classroom had, but it did much more damage. The stripes left her backside much redder and more painful than the last spanking.

When he finished whipping her, she was told to stand in the same spot and to keep her hands off her behind. Her father went outside and came in with two limber switches he had cut from the peach tree in the backyard. He handed Mr. Johnson a ripe peach.

"Bend over again, girl," he said sternly. "It's Daddy's turn now and I won't be so easy on you."

Shelly couldn't seem to stay in position, so Mr. Johnson held her hands and kept her in place. He couldn't stop her screams though, or her tears. When Henry finished switching his daughter's butt and legs, the men ordered her to stand with her face in the corner and her hands off her bottom. They looked over their handiwork with pride. Then by mutual consent, they ordered Shelly to sit on the hard, wooden chair while they turned their harsh attention to her mother.

Mr. Johnson used the switch on Martha with her standing and facing the wall. She was made to hold up her baggy print dress and drop her white cotton panties down on the floor. After Mr. Johnson was done, Henry pulled her over his knees and used a ping pong paddle on her large, solid butt. WHACK! SMACK!

The walloping that the men gave Martha was loud and rowdy but not as hard as Shelly's. It was just hard enough to arouse her. She bore the hard punishment in silence and when it was all over, what she wanted most of all was to get Shelly out of the way and drag her husband to the floor!

"Get your skirt on, girl, and get out of here for a while," she said without taking her wet eyes off her husband. "And take Mr. Johnson with you!"

Shelly made her way slowly and painfully up the stairs and put on a loose, floral skirt. She walked down the stairs and over to the door where her teacher stood waiting. She looked humbly up at Mr. Johnson with a silent question in her eyes.

He met her shy gaze and said, "You do know where we're going and what we're going to do, don't you?" At her bashful nod he continued, "And are you completely sure that it's what you want to do?"

She nodded again with more assurance. "I need to get out of here, and I really need you to hold me and love me."

"I know, little love, come on." He took her hand and led her outside to his car without even a backward glance at her parents. The older couple wouldn't have seen them anyway; Shelly and Mr. Johnson barely got the door closed before Martha had her clothes off and was reaching for her husband. Her butt wasn't too sore for him to fuck her as roughly as he could, right there on the hard, polished wood of the living room floor.

Henry got down onto the floor, shedding his clothes as fast as he could. He rolled over on top of his wife and quickly slid into her. He fucked her with the pent up fury and passion of years. Years of listening to her nag and bitch at him and feeling helpless. Years of denial, of being told that she had a headache, or was not in the mood, or that they were getting to be too old for sex and such foolishness.

In a very short time, Martha realized that they weren't too old. She realized that Henry was a passionate man who had been denied, and she resolved to remember how much she loved him in the future. She returned his passion thrust for thrust and could never remember when she had felt so young and alive, or loved. This time she would work to hold onto it.

Mr. Johnson drove Shelly to his place on the outskirts of town and took her inside. He had a fairly old smaller house, but it was on a large piece of land. The trees that surrounded it gave it a sense of privacy and isolation. As soon as they got inside, he gazed at her tenderly and led her upstairs to his bedroom. They stood next to his king-size bed.

"Get out of those clothes, Shelly, you have another lesson to learn." He started to undress, looking at her with warmth and humor in his eyes. "And you know how much you want to learn it."

Shelly used trembling hands to unbutton her frilly, pink blouse and let it fall to the floor. She slid her floral skirt down and it fell on top of the blouse. She had not bothered to put her panties back on. Mr. Johnson unfastened her lacy bra, cupping her small breasts in his hands. She was naked, but still a little scared and shy.

While Shelly watched, Mr. Johnson paused in undressing, his shirt off and his pants unzipped. She hadn't realized that he had such a muscular body or fine hair on his chest, brown like the hair on his head but not as curly. He walked over to stand behind Shelly and placed his hands gently on her bare, red, throbbing buttocks. He could feel the heat from her whipping.

"It looks painful. If I remember correctly from my boyhood, and somehow I'm sure I do, I know it is painful. We will make it better; do you trust me?" he asked gently.

"I do, for some reason I do but I really don't understand it. Why do I feel this closeness, this trust after what you've done to me?" Shelly turned to look up at him as she asked the question.

"Because what I've done to you was the most intimate and

caring thing that anybody's ever done to you, and because getting a good whipping almost always stirs up a girl's hormones." He reached out a hand and stroked her hair gently, then leaned over and kissed her tenderly on the mouth. "I think it causes the blood to rush to the most sensual areas of the body. Lay down, my little love."

He finished removing his pants and lay down beside her. He began to kiss her very gently, teasing her with his tongue while fondling her breasts with his hands. As she started to respond to the kisses he built the level of passion and intensity, and his hands moved lower down on her slender body.

He began to tease the soft curls and to stroke the tender flesh at the apex of her thighs. She was moaning as he took his mouth from hers to suckle her small firm breasts. She began almost screaming as his mouth went lower still.

By the time he moved over her and started to slide into her, she was more than ready, she was on fire! Her fingernails tore at his shoulders as he ruptured her hymen. She was so aroused that even the momentary pain seemed to further her desire. Shutters began to rack her slender body. He made love to her passionately and furiously, with strong fast thrusts and firm control of her small body. Her scream when she reached orgasm was matched by his own.

Mr. Johnson cuddled her gently for some tender moments, and then got out of bed and went to turn on the shower. He adjusted the water temperature and then came back to the bed. He scooped Shelly up in his strong arms and carried her to the shower. He soaped her gently in the warm spray, easing her sore, aching buttocks. The warm spray loosened up her muscles, muscles that he wanted to make sure would not get stiff from unaccustomed exertion. He used his soapy hands to stimulate her again and rinsed her off before carrying her back to the bed. Once again he made love to her, but this time even more gently and lovingly than before. It was a long time before they were both satisfied, basking side by side in the passionate afterglow.

As he stroked her hair, he asked gently, "Are you all right, little love?"

She smiled at him and replied, "Yes, much better than all right, but I have two questions."

"What are they, my dear?" he asked her gently, his voice full of concern.

She shot him a sly smile and asked, "When can we do this again?"

"Anytime you want, little love, but we have to be careful until school is out next week." He kissed her gently on the forehead. "What's your other question?"

She grinned at him, a grin as full of mischief and wicked humor as any woman ever had, then in a sweet, innocent voice she asked, "What in the hell is your first name?"

I know the teacher/student thing is wrong. I do not believe in teachers either spanking students or having sex with them, but she is over 18 and the story was really fun to write. So what if I'm a bad girl for writing it? Maybe I should be spanked for it. Volunteers?

As a story its got me hot, so far, so good – somebody whip me, please! A hand, a paddle, even a belt would feel so damn good! Oh well, if Mrs. Thumb and her four comely daughters work hard enough, I might get a chapter done in my head, or my lover could come over and do a chapter on my butt. As I sit on this hard, wooden chair I can almost feel the blows.

Seven

Personal: One Tough Customer

*A random encounter with a stranger triggers your most private
fantasy with something silly, say, a T-shirt. Do you follow your
desires and seek him out?*

It was such a classic scenario from a romantic fantasy that Ann
could hardly believe it happened to her; a faceless stranger who
walked into her life and stirred her innermost fantasies and
desires. He was not really a handsome man, but he had an
intriguing, world-weary face. He was older, much older, than any
man who had ever caused her to react so strongly, older than any
man who had ever stimulated her fantasies before. He had gray
hair and weathered skin. Below the sleeves of his T-shirt, she
could see that his well-muscled arms were covered with tattoos.
He should have looked tough and mean, maybe even a little
dangerous, yet somehow he seemed kind, almost gentle.

He wore several turquoise rings and a matching watchband. His
hands were big and the skin was rough looking. There were
calluses on his palms.

He was a character all right, but he wasn't what she would call
sexy. He was just another customer who had come into her
shop, a nice man who wanted to buy some new batteries.

It was his T-shirt that caught Ann's eye. It startled and excited
her. Excited her until she felt her panties get damp. The shirt
had a picture on it. It was a picture of a woman with her bare
butt, bent over enough so that her buttocks were sticking out and
they were shaded slightly pink. The T-shirt read:

~~I~~
~~You~~
We
need a spanking

The words "I" and "You" were crossed out, so the remaining message was: "We need a spanking."

As she rang up his purchase, she felt as if her own butt was tingling all over. Could he tell how affected and aroused she was by his T-shirt? She wanted to ask him if he was a member of one of those sex clubs she'd heard about. The clubs people go to when they want act out sex scenarios on each other. Her slightly puritan side didn't want to let a stranger know about what she still considered to be her dirty little secret, her love of getting and giving spankings, but she knew she couldn't resist. Curiosity killed the cat, she reminded herself, but then she answered back. She was no cat!

It took all her nerve to say anything in front of her nosy male co-worker, a real creep of a computer nerd, but she knew she'd never forgive herself if she didn't. An opportunity like this doesn't come up every day.

She screwed up her courage and said calmly, "Nice shirt. I have a friend who would be really excited by it. He really likes things like that." She hoped she wasn't blushing. "Spanking turns him on."

Ann omitted an explanation about how she knew that her friend was excited about spankings. How she knew that her friend was especially excited about spanking her. She also omitted her own reaction to being spanked, the excitement and anticipation she felt whenever he wanted to spank her. The shivers that ran down her spine when he gave her that certain look, the look that meant a spanking was coming! The thrill she felt when he slid her pants down, whenever he began to stoke her bare bottom, whenever his hand descended in that first, stinging slap.

She knew that the customer wasn't fooled by her evasion when the older man smiled and said, "Your um, friend should come to one of our club meetings. I was at one last night and I had an extraordinarily good time. I got to give lots of good hard spankings to lots of women. And I received a few too. It was fun." He sounded friendly and casual as though it was a completely normal subject to be discussing with a perfect stranger in public.

Ann was filled with a thousand questions. How do you find out about these club meetings? Where are they held? What went on at them? Who could attend? Unfortunately, there was no way she could gather any of this information with her co-worker there, so she let the matter drop. She did however manage to remember his name. That was easy since the man ironically had the same name as a popular movie villain.

A big part of her relationship with Jerry was based on anticipation, caused by the phone calls Jerry made to her. Sometimes he would spend several minutes describing how and what he wanted to do to her. Some of these calls were followed up on when they were together. However some of them were never meant to be reenacted.

One night, Jerry called her up and spent several minutes telling Ann how much his hand ached for the feel of her naked flesh. He described how he wanted to see her skin turn red and hot. When Jerry arrived, Ann was waiting for him, her buttocks tingling with anticipation.

Almost immediately, when he walked in the door, she whispered in his ear, "I need a good, hard spanking, please lover."

Jerry told her to face the sofa and remove her dress, then bend over the back of the sofa as far as she could with her hands on the seat. He walked up behind her and pulled down her pantyhose and noticed at once that her sheer, white underwear had targets embroidered on each side of the bottom, right where his hands would land most often. Since she seldom wore underwear or even hose, he knew this was a deliberate treat planned for him. He also knew that she would be expecting him to react to her targets by giving her an extra harsh spanking.

"I think I'll start by spanking you right over this shameful, decadent underwear," he said in a stern tone. "What kind of a woman puts targets on her underwear? It's shameful! You deserve some punishment, young lady."

Jerry didn't lower her underwear as the spanking began. It was a harsh hand spanking, with long loud cracks as his hand met her butt. The underwear proved to be no protection from the stinging slaps of his hands. In between spanks, he rubbed her butt and legs. Some of his spanks began to land on her bare upper thighs.

"Spread your legs wide and keep them apart," he ordered. "I want to slap the inside of your thighs."

Without a word, Ann complied. The stroking and slapping progressed. Soon her whole bottom was warm and pink from her waist to her knees. Jerry knelt and spanked her calves. He even spanked the soles of her bare feet before working his way back up to the primary target, her full round butt.

Finally, he lowered her underwear and spread a thick layer of cold cream all over her butt before he began to spank her again. It was a long, hard spanking, made even more stinging by the cold cream. For once Jerry scolded her as he spanked her, making her feel like a little girl.

Eventually, inevitably, his hand began to hurt. The spanking stopped and they curled up on the sofa together and watched a movie. The movie ended.

"Bring me the paddle," he ordered sternly.

Ann complied and Jerry had another surprise. She had stored the paddle in the refrigerator, and it was icy cold. She also brought some cold cloths and some ice water.

Jerry had her kneel on the sofa with her butt stuck well up in the air. He used the cool cloths to remove any trace of heat from her behind. Then he picked up the cold paddle and began to beat her soundly with it. Because it was cold, it seemed to take longer to bring the familiar heat to her backside, but the slow steady blows still hurt quite a lot. Finally, when she was squirming and moaning, he poured a little of the ice water on her hot butt and gave her several extra hard smacks with the paddle. The cold was a shock to her system, and the water on her skin made the paddling sting even more. It was glorious agony. All too soon, it was over.

About a week later, the man who Ann privately called "the spanking man" walked into her store again. Ann waited on him, wondering to herself just how a man could use so many batteries. Again her co-worker was at the register when she rang up his purchase, but this time she was lucky as her co-worker walked away to help a customer. "The spanking man" slipped her a piece of paper. He had written down a phone number, an address and a date on a piece of paper and handed it to her quietly. She blushed as she realized that he had come into the store just to give her this piece of paper.

He stared into her eyes. "Will I see you there with your friend?"

She blushed and didn't answer.

"Answer me!" he commanded.

"Yes," Ann replied softly, not meeting his eyes.

"Try saying, 'yes sir,' when you're speaking to someone who's going to take you over his knees and spank you until you cry," he said sternly.

"Yes sir, " Ann whispered.

"I could really do a number on your bottom with these big hands of mine, I could really make your ass sting!" With that he grinned and winked at her and turned and left the shop. "I'll be looking forward to the chance!"

Ann wanted to shout for joy! When she got off work, she laid on the sofa and masturbated while she waited eagerly for her lover to come to her again so she could tell him all about the strange man and the sex club. For once, Jerry disappointed her.

He said, "You should go."

Ann explained that she didn't want to go alone, especially the first time. She used her mouth on Jerry, something she was usually reluctant to do, just to convince him.

Jerry finally agreed when he was able to catch his breath. He also told her that he had a fantasy about sitting back and watching, even directing the action, while she was tied up, gagged and helpless as she was spanked by someone else, by a mysterious stranger. Someone neither one of them had ever met before. Someone neither one of them even knew. This was his chance.

Ann really enjoyed being spanked occasionally, usually just lightly, for kinky fun. Sometimes she liked to take it farther but she always told her lover to stop too soon, and he would always stop when she told him to. She had a fantasy of someone spanking her who wouldn't stop when she said to.

Just once she would like to have someone take her past her limit to the point of her vulnerability. Jerry always stopped when she wanted him to, except for two times, and the memory of those special times was still fresh and exciting.

The first time he failed to stop was the first time he had ever spanked her. It was terrifying, thrilling and very painful. The only other time he spanked her harder than she wanted him to was the only time she had been tied up.

That was the memory that haunted her, excited her. That and the thought of being spanked by a stranger, putting her body into someone else's hands.

What she wanted was to have someone tie her up, and then spank her past the point where she begged him to stop. The person spanking her would listen to her pleas but ignore them, and if he got tired of listening to them he would just gag her and keep going.

Not far past that point, just another six or seven slaps of his hand or blows from the paddle. But those last hits should be the hardest slaps and the sharpest blows. They should be given impersonally, coldly, without regard for her pleas or even her tears. It should feel inevitable.

She wanted the control to be taken out of her hands. She wanted to give herself into someone else's control and possession. Submission. And she wanted to know that the stranger would take her past her personal limit for pain, past her personal point of pleasure, to his or her own satisfaction. She wanted to let it happen with no way of stopping it, no possibility of backing out, no safety net.

She wanted it to hurt, but did not want any severe injuries. She didn't want someone to draw blood or give her any serious bruises. Most important of all, she wanted her lover to be there watching and getting aroused, enjoying her torment, watching her bottom turn red. She wanted to know that her pain was arousing him and that he would fuck her later.

She also wanted to watch him getting spanked, no more than that; she wanted to see him whipped, but she hadn't mentioned that to him yet. Some things should be a surprise.

Nervously, they walked into the club. Ann was in her tight black slacks and her new black sweater with gold threading. Jerry was in blue work pants and a striped polo shirt. Ann was conflicted and half of her wanted to back out; she felt apprehensive, agitated, aroused and wet. She was humiliated because she didn't have any sexy lingerie on, but her lover told her that any lingerie would be removed anyway, so that she could be spanked on her bare bottom. So who cared?

Somehow that thought wasn't particularly comforting or reassuring. Ann gathered her nerve and told herself that if she wanted something comforting or reassuring she wouldn't be here, would she?

Ann looked around the room. It was a large meeting hall with several small rooms off to one side. There were chairs around the outside of the room and some ominous-looking contraptions in the center. Although people were still arriving, there was already a woman was getting spanked across a man's knees.

Ann quickly found out that she enjoyed watching someone else being spanked, even knowing that she would soon be getting spanked herself.

Jerry roamed the room and joined in several conversations. For a while she thought her lover was trying to talk a woman into spanking her, but he was just making idle conversation. The idea seemed a little bizarre to her. She had never even thought about it. She let the idea sink in; she could be spanked by a woman just as well as a man. Finally she realized, who cares what sex the person beating you is? The person doing the spanking is unimportant; they are just an instrument in your desire for punishment, like the paddle itself.

The person doing the beating is not a sex partner. The sex partner would be her lover, the watcher. Whatever she felt, whatever happened to her, no matter whose hands held the paddle, it would be him beating her. Loving her. Spanking her. His eyes on her, arousing her. Him.

Her lover wound up talking to the man she had met at the shop. He still seemed like a nice, friendly man. He was a big, burly, middle-aged man. He had a weather-beaten face, graying hair and large, solid hands still sporting the turquoise rings. He was still not her normal fantasy man, but nevertheless, she had fantasized about him for weeks. Her lover told him what they wanted, how long and hard. The older man looked to her for confirmation.

Her voice was soft and shaky as she said, "Yes, I want you to spank me and then use a paddle on me with my lover watching. I want it to be as hard and as long as he told you. The only thing I don't want is any of the insults or humiliation crap that sometimes seems to go with discipline. I want to be treated nicely, with basic courtesy, even while I'm being tied up. And the most important thing I want is to have the final say about how long the punishment is going to last or how hard I'm going to be hit, taken entirely out of my hands. After all, it's none of my damn business."

Her asking for it, telling this man how to beat her was a very important and exciting part of the experience. "I want it to hurt a lot and I want it to be on my naked butt."

The man nodded and said simply, "Okay girl. This is it. Off with your pants."

She was shocked! There were people all around them. She thought it would happen in a side room with some privacy. She sent him a wide-eyed look and he just smiled and raised an eyebrow. He stood there with his arms crossed over his large chest. Without another word, she lowered her eyes demurely and took off her slacks.

The man said one more word, "Underwear."

Just one word. She swallowed hard, looking at her lover. It was happening! Suddenly she was in a panic, her stomach seemed to be filled with butterflies. Slowly, almost reluctantly, she obeyed. The man took her hand and led her to a small room and told her to bend over a padded rail. Her lover helped the man as he strapped her to it tightly, hands and feet.

The man asked, "Last chance, tell me now. You want it for real? You want it hard? You want it to hurt? And you don't want me to stop when you beg me to?"

She answered honestly, but nervously, "Yes, for real, hard and painful, and past the point where I say stop." She paused. "Just don't go too far, you'll know when to stop. I'm putting my trust in you."

He began with his hand; not too hard but firm, solid slaps, all on her left cheek. They felt terrific and sounded even better. CRACK! He did her right cheek. Then he spanked her left cheek again, harder and a little faster. He covered the whole area of her bottom, even going down to the tops of her thighs. The right again. She squirmed.

He gave her a good long warm up before he picked up a leather strap. He started slowly with the strap but it really stung. The severity and speed of the smacks built up then eased off. Over and over, he built it up, and then eased off. Sometimes, when he was going easy on her, he would land one sharp hard blow. Still, he continued.

She tried to keep quiet but finally the words came pouring out. "STOP! ENOUGH!" He paused for an instant. She relaxed, then he hit her with six of the hardest blows yet on her left cheek. She squirmed and yelled. He stopped again, waiting for her to force herself to relax, then did the same to her right cheek. He left her tied up and walked away.

Her lover stroked and kissed her hot behind, nipping it, loving it. He enjoyed the warmth and color of it. Without any warning he blindfolded her, causing her to feel even more helpless and somehow naked and unprotected. It was as if she was on display for all the members to see. If anyone walked by, he asked them if they wanted to give her ass a slap. Several people did; the slaps were sharp and unexpected, and great. She was left like that for almost an hour. Her wrists were numb and her back was sore from bending. She wanted to be let up, but she wanted the rest of it, the pain that was still coming.

The man came back with the heavy paddle. For once, she would feel what it was like to be paddled with something that wasn't a ping pong paddle or a cutting board. It was a real paddle. It was long and thick, and it had holes drilled into the surface in order to stop the wind resistance to make it hurt more. It was meant for only one purpose: to beat and punish the human butt.

He only said one word. "Ready?"

For several minutes he held the paddle against her ass, just held it there. Finally he began to use the paddle on her, loud and hard, each blow spaced out for just a second, to let the feeling soak in. The pain, the sting. No slow build up this time, it was harsh from the start.

A group was watching and she began to act up for the crowd. She exaggerated her very real gasps and moans. She squirmed as much as the straps would allow.

She tried not to say stop, but finally she screamed the word, "Stop!"

The man stopped instantly, only to start again after putting a gag in her mouth.

Some of the people in the crowd complained that he was supposed to stop when she said to quit. Her lover explained to the onlookers that it was agreed beforehand that the man would not stop. He gave her six more harsh, stinging blows on each side, then stopped. She relaxed, and he suddenly gave her six more across the center. These last blows landed on both cheeks at once. They were very hard and very fast. Each one sounded like a gunshot in the small room. It was over. Finally.

Her lover put a cool damp cloth on her butt, then untied her. He ordered her not to put her pants back on, but instead to just lay face down on the sofa.

For the next hour or so, she laid there naked from the waist down so that anyone could see and stroke, and even slap her hot red butt. She had no say in the matter. If someone asked her lover, he would tell them to go ahead and give her a slap or two.

She found out that her lover was going to pay the man back for her beating by spanking him. She got up and pulled her pants back into place. She walked over and watched, thinking it was a little funny to see her lover spanking this bigger, tougher, older man. A slender young woman Ann had never met before came up to her, slapped her sore butt right over her pants, and then they started talking.

The woman had a cat o' nine tails in her hand. She told Ann to drop her pants, bend over and grab the seat of a chair. Ann did, and the woman whipped her for several minutes with the cat, but not especially hard. Ann stood up and raised her pants.

Then the woman asked Ann to use it on her, only longer and harder. They traded positions and Ann whipped the woman, swinging the cat hard, giving her about a dozen harsh slashing strokes.

When Ann's lover finished beating her former harsh disciplinarian and came back over to her, he bent over, pulled her pants down partly and kissed her still flaming ass. The woman asked him if he would like to be beaten with a cat o' nine tails.

Ann's lover looked surprised and more than a little bit apprehensive, but she answered for him. "Of course he would! Unless he's too scared?"

Her lover shot her an icy glare and whispered, "Wait until I get you home."

"What are you going to do? Beat me?" Ann teased. "Big deal, it's way too late for that to be any real threat!"

Jerry lowered his pants and laid himself over the rail. Ann told the woman that her lover liked to be hit really, really hard, but he didn't see her give the woman a wink. He started to protest but she turned her back to him and dropped her pants so that he could see her red ass. It worked. He took one look at the marks on her butt and kept his mouth shut.

The woman whipped him more for show than to hurt him, but it was hard enough to sting and make him suck in his breath a couple of times. Ann took the cat from the woman and whipped him six very severe cuts to finish him off.

She walked around for a while and some people gave her a friendly slap or two. Her lover got paddled by another older woman while Ann sat gingerly on a hard wooden chair and watched, sipping champagne. Although she was no longer naked from the waist down, Ann almost felt as if she were. Her bottom was still red and very sore.

Later as she walked around, a strange middle-aged man came up to her and said, "I can tell that you were a very, very bad girl, a very wicked girl. Drop your pants. Face the wall and brace yourself, hands about waist high."

She obeyed instantly, and he gave her a harsh little butt warmer: long, hard and fast with his bare hand and a paddle he had with him. She thanked him for taking the time to punish her so severely and she kissed his hand.

Finally, the meeting ended. Ann found her lover, Jerry, and they went home.

At home, her lover looked at her butt again, noticing the blotches and bruises. He questioned her about whether she had enjoyed the punishment. He asked her if she could stand another spanking before they went to bed.

Ann didn't bother answering his question; she just lay down on the sofa and buried her face in her arms and waited...

My ass is cold. I need to be spanked hard. That's what I get for breaking up with my lover. Now I have to find a new lover and train him to fulfill my desires, and learn to fulfill his. Hey, this could be exciting! Actually, my butt hurts just from reading this.

Eight

Cindy's Spanking

A modern woman goes into a coma and dreams of herself as Cinderella. What does she do? Well, after she does the morning chores she goes for a peaceful swim. She also wonders to herself why Cinderella was such a wimp and lets herself be ordered around. Her Prince is not so charming. He has a temper...

After she pitched the ashes and the contents of the chamber pot over the ledge, she carried the buckets over to the stream and left them there.

As always, she had climbed the hill and thrown the ashes and waste off the bluff, a short distance behind her house. It was something she did without thought, something she did everyday, something she thoroughly hated having to do. She closed off her mind and strove to close off her sense of smell. She just blindly threw the contents of the pots into the breeze off the cliff.

There were several things Cindy didn't know. How could she know?

How could she know that today would be different? That today, doing the detested chore, would lead to disaster? To a fateful meeting that could deflect her anger towards her family and even change her life? How could she know that anyone was riding along the road just below the steep bluff?

She certainly didn't know that the cliff she emptied the buckets from was within range of the road far below when the wind conditions were just right.

And how could she know that of all the people who might be riding there as she emptied out the ashes, it would be the young Prince out riding on his great warhorse? How could she know that he was in a fierce mood already?

She didn't know that the Prince and his two guards ever rode along that road, let alone that they were there that very day. She didn't know that the Prince had a quick temper, especially when he felt slighted in front of any of his men. And she certainly didn't know that some of the ashes and even a few drops of the other waste had landed on him.

Nothing that happened was her fault in any way. She just wanted to get to the pond in time for her swim before she had to return to start the evening chores.

Humming to herself, she followed the path and the stream down to a small, clear pond. Looking around quickly, she saw no one. She disrobed, hung her grubby dress on a nearby branch and leapt into the pond. The water felt cool and wonderful. She felt so relaxed and free. Swimming was one of the many pleasures Cindy's stepmother, Gertrude, denied her. It was not from any concern or love of Cindy, but from fear that if Cindy drowned, she and her daughters may actually have to do the chores themselves.

Still, it seemed that the world was so beautiful and peaceful that she felt she could truly relax and enjoy the pleasant interlude.

She was wrong. Very, very wrong.

So Cindy swam, relaxed and tranquil, not knowing that her idyll was about to come to an abrupt end.

It so happened that it was a terrible day for Cindy's carelessness. The Prince was already in a bad mood before ever having the ashes blown into his face. The ashes escalated his bad mood into outright anger when he felt the first droplets hit his velvet riding coat. He had looked up in time to see the chamber pot being emptied. The anger turned into a white-hot fury. He quickly kicked his great black warhorse into a gallop to get away from the foul mess but in truth, not many drops could have reached him even if he had stood his ground. He was really quite far from the person emptying the waste.

Angered, the Prince rode quickly to find out who had committed such an insult to his royal person. He was not usually an unjust or unreasonable man but on this day he was in a foul mood. His father, King Nigel, and his mother, Queen Dorthea, were demanding that he marry, and he was not yet ready to give up his freedom for the chains of a wife and children, or for the added responsibilities of the kingdom his father wanted him to assume.

The only reason he was out riding at all that day was to escape his royal mother's nagging tongue. He dearly loved the woman but he had to admit, she could bring a saint to his knees with the rough side of her tongue. She was utterly relentless! He had ridden hard to escape the guards who were assigned to ride with him, for he dearly wanted some time to himself, even a few timeless moments. However even that was denied him, for his guards were close by. They were true and loyal to the Prince but they answered to the King and Queen.

He wanted to soothe his temper with some peace and quiet, and some rare, precious solitude. He understood his parents concern. He was the only Prince and his parents wanted him to marry and produce heirs to the throne while they were still alive.

Part of what riled him so much was their unspoken fear that if he were to meet an untimely end without issue, they would have no one to succeed themselves as King and Queen, and the kingdom would pass away from their family. It was vaguely unsettling to realize that his parents feared for his mortality. The fact that they feared out of concern for the kingdom instead of from their love for him only chafed him even more. If he had not been so irked by his mother's nagging he would have admitted to himself that he knew they did, indeed, worry for him out of love, as any parents worry for their child. On this day however, he was too irritated and upset to think rationally. And that was before he was hit with the ashes and the contents of the chamber pot.

His smoldering temper burst into full flame as he sought out the villain who had covered him with ashes and piss, especially since the ashes were making him sneeze. Sneezing always made the young Prince feel so undignified and common.

It was a long sweeping path around the bluffs to the point

where the ashes and disgusting waste had come from. It was also too narrow and steep to safely travel at a full gallop. Even though he hurried, it took him almost a quarter hour to reach the top of the bluff. By the time the Prince found the tiny stone cottage tucked away in the overgrown woods, there was no one to be seen.

Cindy had finished her chores for the moment, and she was doing something wild and wicked. Something just a little daring. She was swimming naked in the pond, really relaxing for the first time in days. There she was alone, free and, for once, no one was yelling at her. That is no one yelled at her until the Prince came upon her and asked if she knew who the fool was that was throwing all kinds of foul matter on the future King.

She hunched down under the water and looked up into angry green eyes and defiantly told him that if he got filth all over his royal self, it was his own royal fault.

It was unfortunate for her that she was naked. Unfortunate that she was feeling defiant, that she was not in a mood to let herself be yelled at by anybody, royal Prince or not, no matter how handsome he was. Unfortunate that the Prince was in one of his very rare foul moods. Such a foul mood that he barely noticed her beauty. He barely noticed the delicacy of her features. He paid no attention to the creamy softness of her skin. He never saw the full thrust of her bare breasts as he rode his horse right into the pond and reached down to pull the furiously struggling, naked girl out of the water. He lifted her up and dragged her across his horse's back. He placed her so that she was draped across the hard cantle of his saddle; her head was hanging down by the foreleg of his great warhorse, and the ends of her long hair were flowing in the water.

She was off balance; her buttocks were straight up in the air and she was draped too far over the horse's withers to stay in place without the prince holding her firmly in position. The feel of the saddle beneath her was uncomfortable. She was furious, indignant and terrified.

In spite of her struggling and wiggling, he managed her quite easily. Holding her in place with one large hand, he spanked her bare bottom with the other.

It was a long, hard spanking. His hand rose and fell in a relentless rhythm. The heavy black leather riding glove he wore made a loud smacking sound as it landed on her wet butt, and each blow really stung. He alternated cheeks but landed the blows on the same area of each cheek. The pain of those two large, bright red spots was intense. This was not a playful romp; it was a real spanking meant to punish, and punish it did. He was so involved in spanking her that he never heard his two guards ride up. He never heard their laughter, but she did. It added to her anger and humiliation.

He just continued spanking her. He didn't leave her with any bruises but he did cause her bottom to turn bright red and flaming hot. Because the heavy gloves protected his hands, he was hitting her even harder than he realized. She was very red and had two large splotches, one on each cheek. Finally he stopped. He held her for a moment while she continued to struggle. She was conscious of her flaming, aching bottom and also of the discomfort from her position on the horse. She felt the rough texture of the horse's mane, the boniness of his withers, along with the hard leather of the cantle of the prince's saddle, and the rough cloth of his breeches. Finally she quieted.

Disdainfully, he dropped her back into the shockingly cool water. He glanced at her as she shivered with the jolt of cold water on her flaming butt and realized that she was indeed, a very comely maid.

She had a firm body with perfect skin and full thrusting breasts. They looked even larger and more luscious because she was heaving with anger. The nipples were tipped with a dusky rose tint, and tightened by the cold water into tight little buds. Seeing his gaze, she turned her back to him. Her long wet hair was streaming over her soft shoulders. She had a tiny waist, gently flared hips and round firm buttocks, now turned dark red, with purple bruises showing in the center of each cheek.

She looked up over her shoulder at him with bright blue eyes, shiny with tears she struggled to hold back. Her defiance and outrage were barely held in check. In spite of her anger, she felt a thrill course through her veins at the sight of the young Prince. His black hair was pulled back into a queue and his brilliant green eyes flared with an unnamed emotion. He was wearing a black velvet riding coat trimmed with gold braid and had on a green vest. His shirt was pure white linen with a froth of lace at the collar and cuffs. He was wearing snug, russet breeches and, against her will, her vision was drawn to the bulge of his manhood straining against the tightness of his crotch.

They both stood there, silent and still, for a long moment before he reached down and once again dragged her out of the water. He pulled her into his arms and kissed her. It was no tender, tentative, gentle first kiss like a gentleman should give an innocent maid. It was not a lover's kiss, tender but coaxing ever more passion. It was an insulting and demanding kiss with thrusting tongue and hard, intense lips. The passion in it was full-blown and instantaneous. She struggled briefly before succumbing to the passion and ardor of the kiss. Her senses were filled with him. His hand started to slide towards her breast and the kiss seemed to go on forever before the Prince heard someone calling his name. It was one of his guards! The man was laughing!

"Your Highness, do you want us to lose ourselves again?" the guard asked. "Or should we drag this creature back to the castle for you?"

The Prince broke off the kiss abruptly, barely avoiding her slap. "What? What would I want with her at the castle?"

"Well, when we first saw you with her you seemed to be intent on beating her black and blue," the guard said slowly. "Did she mayhap commit some insult on your royal person? We could have her beheaded if you wish."

"He dinna look to me like he wanted her beheaded," the other guard said. "He looked like he just wanted her bedded."

"The Prince interested in a girl?" the first guard jested. "'Tis the Queen who would want the girl at the palace."

"The Queen wants to see me in love and married," the Prince said softly. "She knows I bed the lasses, but she wants to see me tied to just one and producing heirs."

"So if this girl has caught your eye," the first guard said with an open grin, "the Queen would want to know about it. In the space of a heartbeat she would have a priest ready to join you to the lass, whoever she is."

"Even the Queen wants to be sure the girl I wed is worthy," the Prince said. "Not a common strumpet such as this."

He stole another passionate kiss and avoided another attempted slap before dropping her into the cool water once again. Without a word he kicked his horse and rode off in a splash of water followed by a cloud of dust. He left behind an intrigued and angry woman. A woman who had been pushed around far too many times, threatened far too many times, and who worked far too hard. Now, her anger and frustration at all the wrongs in her life had a focus. She was bent on seeing him again. For revenge. Only for revenge.

Is it really revenge our Cindy is after? Is that what she gets? This is a mere glimpse of a forthcoming romance novel, <u>Just Another Sleeping Beauty</u>. The big question is: why does the book have the words 'sleeping beauty' in the title when it's about Cinderella?

Nine

Mucho Macho Man

This is a fairly real story about one of the parties I go to, or one of the ones I host myself. We have fun. We have a real sense of friendship, but we also have our romances. I am so proud of the way our group treats newbies; they go out of their way to make them feel welcome and at ease. Of course, they also go out of their way to make sure the new tops get to play. And of course, to make sure the new bottoms are treated very warmly. In fact, by they time they leave, they are usually more than warm, they are red hot!

The people on my list, and spankos in general, are the best people I know. This story is for them. Two men in particular.

His name was Sean. He was in his mid-thirties and had dark blond hair that had been streaked by the sun. He was fairly tan, and very fit; not overtly muscular, but taut and strong. His face was slightly weathered and angular. His eyes were stern, dark piercing blue. Overall, he was handsome, tough and very masculine. That's how the new member looked to the spanking group when he arrived at his first party.

No one knew much about him, or how he had learned about the group. No one knew if Sean was his real name. They didn't even know what he did for a living. That was normal in the group. He seemed to have nice clothes and a good car, so he was probably doing okay, but no one really cared. In this group personality counted the most, with looks and money pretty far down the list.

The women in the group, single or married, felt a flutter as they secretly studied the new man. The married women just did a better job of keeping that flutter hidden. They might admire and

107

play with a new man, but they also respected their husbands.

Sean sat and talked with the members and most of them took an instant liking to the man. He was pleasant, intelligent and had a real sense of humor. He didn't seem to feel awkward or nervous like some newbies did. He seemed completely at ease and fit in very well.

He heard people asking each other if they wanted to play, and then saw them disappear into a bedroom. He heard the distinctive sound of a spanking follow these disappearances. He quietly asked the lady next to him, who he'd been chatting casually with, if she wanted to play. He was pleased when she said yes.

He was shocked when she turned to him as they walked to the bedroom. "I don't play very hard," she said, "unless I've played a lot. I play more for fun, and I use code words. You know, red means stop and yellow means ease up."

She said as she climbed on the bed and laid face down. "Is this okay or do you want me over your knees?"

He was fairly new to spanking, although for years he had fantasized about being spanked. He was, at heart, a true bottom. He had never had any thoughts about being a top. He had played privately with a former girlfriend, but she was a vanilla woman. She agreed to spank him but really didn't enjoy it. She certainly would not have let him spank her, even if he had asked. He had never switched. The same thing happened with all the women he wanted to play with. They all seemed to assume he was a top. He tried to play with them the way they wanted, but it was uncomfortable for him and the women.

"He is soooooo hot," one woman said to another. "Too bad he's no good at it."

"Something is definitely wrong," she agreed. "No one could look that good, be a spanko, and be so uncomfortable with the whole thing. He asked me to play and then when we got to the bed, he seemed reluctant."

"Yeah," a third woman chipped in, "it's not like we dragged him kicking and screaming into the bedroom."

He left the party fairly early, and very disappointed.

Shortly after the party there was a party report on the groups list, describing the fun and games. It was followed by another post:

> *"I'm fairly new to the scene and I have some questions. How do I ask someone to play? If I'm a bottom, I mean. I went to a party a few weeks ago, and when I asked women to play with me, they draped themselves over my lap, without finding out if I wanted to spank them or have them spank me. What did I do wrong?"*

A couple of weeks ago my ass, Sheila thought, this is from that new guy last Friday. No wonder he was such a bad spanker.

She posted a reply:

> *"I'm sorry you had a bad time at your first party. You make a good point, we should not assume whether you are a bottom or a top. You are an adult though, and you should be able to tell the person you want to play with what you want. Maybe it's hard to say you want a spanking, it can be hard for me as a woman, so maybe it's even harder for a man.*
>
> *If you are the person I think you are, then I met you at the party. I'm a switch so I would have been more than glad to top you. I would have loved to see you drop your pants and to have your bottom at my mercy. I would have spanked you like the bad boy you are. I would have turned that bottom a bright, hot red. I would have... well, you get the picture. Next time, I will. I promise. You may regret that promise when I get my hands on you.*
>
> *You might want to consider learning to switch. Not if the idea repulses you of course, since we believe in consensual play, but just in the spirit of expanding your horizons. If you tell your partner that you're a bottom who wants to learn to top, they will be patient and help you learn. It's all about giving pleasure. I only say this because I started off as a pure bottom about 5 years ago and now there are many men out there who would be surprised to learn that, and there are more than a few who might wish I had never learned to top."*

Sheila's reply struck a note with him. It was not the only reply by far, but it made him take notice. He got many replies; some not so nice, and some very hot. He was sympathized with, teased and insulted. Some were sent off list, but most were posted to the group list. The gist of it was:

> *"If you want to be spanked, for goodness sakes, let us know! We aren't mind readers."*

One woman simply said:

> *"Speak up next time, I don't work for Psychic Friends. You're gonna get it now, Bud!"*

He wasn't sure if he was eager or afraid to go to the next party. He even thought about topping, or giving pleasure, as Sheila put it. How hard could it be to learn? He thought, the hand goes up and down, over and over.

He arrived at the next party just as things were warming up. Well, just as a few bottoms were being warmed up. He was surprised to learn that many of the group members didn't mind if he watched as they played. Why hadn't he noticed that the first time? He realized that at the first party he was more concerned with making a good impression than learning how to truly fit in. That was his first mistake.

The group knew, of course, that he was the one who had posted on list about being a bottom. They weren't stupid people. No one said anything to him about it though; they just accepted him as one of them. He watched two women top a man, taking turns spanking him, and using various toys: straps, paddles, a cane and even some feathers!

They chatted gaily with the man and with each other, thoroughly enjoying themselves. It was a strange but very real sense of teamwork and camaraderie between the two women. They were having a great time!

The man seemed to be able to take an enormous amount of

spanking. His bottom was scarlet and splotchy but he was relaxed, goading them on to even greater severity.

"Have you started yet?" he asked the women. It got a big response; a torrent of very hard blows rained down on his bare buttocks.

Sean asked and learned that he had been slowly warmed up. He also learned that the man had been into the scene for years and both women knew him well and had played with him often.

"You hit like girls," he said to the women.

Again his smart mouth got him a real response. His butt was like leather.

The man, talking even as he was face down getting caned, explained that they would go easier on a newbie, learning what he liked and what his limits were. They would also take time with a warm up.

As the two women finished with him, he introduced Sean to the women. One was a tall, regal beauty named Suzanne, and Sean learned that the majestic looking woman was married to a man named James.

James was the current president of *The Paddle Club*, a group that met monthly in a private mansion about 25 miles away. She promptly invited him to come to a meeting, promising to email him the directions and time, along with a few more facts about the club.

The other woman, a short perky brunette was Sheila. She was about thirty, plump and curvy, but not fat. She had laughing brown eyes.

"Pleased to meet you Sean," Sheila said, "especially since I owe you one truly memorable spanking. It happens now."

"What?" Sean was surprised.

"Drop your jeans and get face down on that bed, and I do mean now!" The change from laughing imp to severe dom was so swift it shocked Sean, but her tone allowed no leeway, no room for trying to squirm out of the promised spanking. In truth, Sean wanted no way out. He was ready!

He reached for the zipper of his jeans. Feeling suddenly

awkward, he lowered the pants down around his ankles and laid himself across the bed. Sheila began spanking him, not very hard, but with quick slaps covering the whole area of his bottom. She was talking to him the whole time, telling him to speak out if things got too hard or if he wanted to stop.

She picked up the strength and speed of the spanks, slowly but surely. She stopped and picked up a small wooden paddle. She paddled him sharply for several minutes. His bottom tingled, but so far there had been no real pain. It hardly felt like a spanking at all. He struggled to hide his disappointment.

"Okay, that's enough pampering." She reached for the waistband of his jockey shorts. "Let's get down to business. Okay?"

At his quick nod, she pulled his shorts down and suddenly he knew that as far as she was concerned, warm up was over. Completely. Whap! The paddles cracked down on his naked ass. And emphatically! Whap! Over! Oh my God, she had a strong swing. Whap! She was vicious with the paddle. Whap! It went on and on. Whap!

Suddenly she put down the paddle. In spite of the fact that this was exactly the spanking he had dreamed of, he tensed, waiting to see what she did next. She paused, lightly stroking his buttocks using her acrylic nails to gently rake his enflamed skin. The sensations were incredible. She teased him gently for short time while deciding what toy to use next on his naughty bottom. She decided on a heavy leather strap.

Crack! He almost shot off the bed, surprised at how the strap felt. From the first, each blow was harsh and heavy, coming quickly. There was no let up for a long time. He endured this in silence; right, for about ten seconds he did, then he started to gasp, squirm, and yell.

"Owwww! Ouch dammit!" he shouted.

"Ouch is not a code word," she replied, without letting up in the least.

"Son of a bitch!" he yelled with emotion.

"I'm nobody's son, fella," she said grimly, "and that's not the code either."

And still she swung the strap. It was a very long time before she stopped. A very long time before she teased him again. By now a crowd was watching.

Although watching was permitted, at least some of the time, it was only with the consent of the people playing. This particular group liked to do more than just watch, they were fond of putting in their two cents worth of ribald remarks, off-color comments and helpful suggestions.

Most of the group had seen many spankings and usually they were too busy talking and feeding their faces to stop and watch. This time, because of the curiosity his post had aroused, there were big mouth spectators crowded into the bedroom.

"I guess that he's not going to complain about being a top again," one woman said.

"Being a top sounds pretty good right about now," he laughed, surprising himself.

"Yeah, and remember Suzanne still has a score to settle with him," someone said, laughing. "He's in trouble now."

"Suzanne?" He was shocked.

"Does the phrase, 'You're gonna get it now, bud,' ring any bells?" Suzanne said sweetly.

"No. Gee, I'm sorry I can't place that phrase," he said, obviously lying. "I must have forgotten it."

"When Sheila's done, I'm sure I can refresh your memory," Suzanne said laughing.

"Why wait?" Sheila laughed. "Grab a pair of wooden spoons and we can have some fun playing percussion."

It was his last warning. Soon both women were each using two wooden spoons like drumsticks. Suzanne on his right cheek and Sheila on his left. Those women had a real sense of rhythm, but their competition got in the way. The drummers got faster and faster, building to a frenzied crescendo. He let them know how much he appreciated their effort with his yelling and gasps. He even had a hard time staying in place. The one thing he did not do was ask them to stop, or use the code words.

Again there was a pause for tickling, gentle stroking, and teasing. They stroked, rubbed and tickled him from his throbbing bottom to the soles of his feet, but they never put their hands in any private places, whether he wanted them to or not. The two women rubbed cool lotion onto his hot bottom.

One of the spectators said, "They must be done now."

"Yeah, probably," someone replied. "They usually don't rub the lotion on until they're done because it makes the spanking sting more when the skin has just been covered with lotion."

He began to relax until he realized that both women were each picking up still another paddle. He soon learned the unseen spectator was dead on right – it did sting more. That didn't stop the dynamic duo; they paddled, strapped and spanked until their arms were tired.

As they put the last paddle down, Sheila asked aloud, "I wonder which one of us is better with the cane?"

"Let's find out," Suzanne laughed, an almost wicked laugh. "We can judge by the screams."

Well, he didn't actually scream but some of the sounds he made came damned close. The spectators gave Sheila the nod as the best with a cane. Sean, perhaps wisely, had no comment. God forbid Suzanne demand a rematch! He got off the bed and gave both women a hug and his thanks.

"You may give our host a run for the money as champion 'leather butt' of the group," one woman said. "That was one hell of a spanking you took."

"Hey!" the host called out. "I'm still the champion. No damned newbie is gonna take my title!"

"We could have a spank-off to decide," someone said with exaggerated innocence.

"No thanks all the same," Sean said, laughing. "I'd be honored just to be the runner-up in that category."

Most of the group, Sean and Sheila included, went back to the living room and dove hungrily into the pizzas that had just been delivered. Sean almost blushed when he realized the pizza delivery boy must have heard his spanking. Then he learned that the pizza delivery boy was a part of the group, and would be back to play as soon as his shift was over.

After eating, which he managed to sit down for, he walked over to talk with Sheila.

"Would you still be willing to teach me to top?" he asked with his own version of a wicked grin.

"Sure," she smiled openly back at him. "I have some questions though. First, did you like the spanking we gave you? Was it too hard? Not hard enough?"

"It was perfect," he told her with a wide grin. "I loved it. I did come close to saying the code word but I never had to. Just about when I thought I couldn't take any more, you eased off."

"I know the signs pretty well," she admitted. "Also, why do you want to learn to top? Is it to get a bit of revenge?"

"Revenge?" He was surprised. "Hell, no! I just have a sudden desire to have your bare bottom at my control."

"And you do realize that I don't play as hard as you do?" Was her final question.

"Yes, of course," he said with exaggerated innocence. "I would never want to spank you too hard."

"Yeah, I believe that," Sheila laughed. "Not!"

She looked at him and smiled. The she stood, held out her hand to him and said, "Okay, let's play."

With her coaching, although topping from the bottom was sometimes frowned upon, and some help from the party's host, he gave her a very satisfactory spanking. It lasted a long time, interspersed with lots of rubbing and teasing. He spanked her hard enough to make her squirm, but not too hard for her to enjoy it. He used a lot of different toys and learned a lot about each one. He found out that he really enjoyed topping, and he liked the scenery too. Naked female backsides at his disposal, how cool is that?

As they walked back to their cars after the party, he asked her out, suggesting dinner and a movie the next evening. She quickly said yes. She was no fool; this man was seriously hot, a spanko, potentially a great spanko and really nice. She gave him her phone number and address. They shared a hug and a quick kiss goodnight.

Dinner the next night was a perfect date. They enjoyed the restaurant and talked a lot, about everything. They found out they had a lot in common besides spanking.

They liked the same foods. They enjoyed the same movies and also watched the same TV shows. They followed the same sports, but rooted for different teams. Both of them loved horses and they were both dog people; neither particularly liked cats.

After they went to a movie, he took her home and kissed her gently at the door. One kiss led to two, and the second had more heat to it. That kiss led to one with more passion, and then it wasn't enough, for either of them. She invited him in for some coffee, which didn't get made until breakfast the next morning. They spent the next day, Sunday, together. That first date ended Monday morning, depressingly early, because he had to leave early to get ready for work.

At the next few parties they arrived together, and when they left, they went to her apartment and played a different game, although as with the spanking, the game usually took place in her bedroom. Even in that, they were more than compatible, they were combustible.

They were often seen at *The Paddle Club* as well as at many of the private parties in the area. They were a popular couple, well-liked and fun to play with. He showed real talent as a top, but still preferred to bottom.

Before the year was out they got married. They had two ceremonies. One was traditional, simple and beautiful. Like all 'simple' weddings, it took slightly more planning than the invasion at Normandie. It cost a king's ransom and turned Sheila into a bridezilla. The second ceremony for the spankos was truly simple, filled with humor, spankings and love.

I have invited anyone who inquired about the parties to come to one, with very few exceptions: The inquiries coming from people who seem to think a spanking party is another word for an orgy, and the ones who seem to really want to inflict pain, without limits. Our spanking parties are for consensual spankings, without any other form of BDSM.

The amazing thing is, with only one or two exceptions in over five years, I have had very few guests that didn't fit in with the group. Almost 100% of the newbies turn out to be real assets to the group.

Ten

It's Never Too Late

In this one a name was changed to protect the not-so-innocent. I know he won't really be flattered to be named after a talking horse, but it really was the better of two choices. I kept thinking of Francis the Talking Mule, but I didn't want his nickname to be Jackass. Although sometimes, my dear friend, if the nickname fits... LOL

Alycia sat in front of her computer reading the emails posted at her favorite "guilty pleasure" web site. It was a group called Santa Del Rio Spanking. Her fascination was not based on her being a part of the spanking scene; she was what they called a "lurker." She never posted to the group, only read their emails. She never went to one of their parties either. In fact, she'd never even been spanked.

It's just that she was intrigued by the idea of a pleasure spanking; more than just intrigued, she was almost obsessed by the idea. Spanking had been a secret fantasy of hers for as long as she could remember.

The Internet group seemed so different than what she expected. She thought a group of "Spankos" as they sometimes called themselves would be, she sighed to herself and thought, even in her own mind she was struggling for the right words: cruder, more abusive towards women and more secretive. That was what she thought; that the spankos would be more demeaning and obnoxious than this particular group sounded. This group sounded friendly, warm and inviting.

They talked about spanking as if it were a normal everyday pastime, thoroughly enjoyable for both parties, even the one on the receiving end. From their posts, she learned that it wasn't

118

always women being spanked and men doing the spanking. They talked quite a bit about limits, safety words and making sure everyone felt safe and comfortable, and that they were not pressured into "playing" as they called it. She just read the posts, but she read enough to know that what she was doing was called lurking because she was only reading and not participating in the discussions; not quite ready to jump in and become active on the list.

"Oh well, it's never too late," she thought. "Maybe if I finish doing this favor for Miguel, he'll listen to me about my interests for once and go to a munch with me. There's even one tomorrow, at some place fairly nearby called the barn."

Deep inside she knew it would never happen; Miguel thought the only way a real man would hit a woman was with his fists or a fast hard slap across the face. Somewhere deep inside she knew that she should leave Miguel forever, but she just couldn't seem to do it. She just kept putting it off.

The phone rang, it was Miguel. "Are you ready?" he asked without even a greeting.

"Yes, Miguel," she replied softly, reluctantly.

"Do you know what to do?" he said curtly.

"Yes, Miguel, but I don't think I… " she began.

"Don't think at all, you stupid bitch, just do as I say," he shouted.

It was the last straw. "Yes Miguel, but this is the last time I'll do it. I know that what's in those packages is something that could get me into trouble. How stupid do you think I am?" she shouted back. "I will never do this for you again, and I will never let you speak to me that way again. This is it!" She practically spat at the phone. "After tonight, we're through."

She never realized how prophetic that statement was, not until much later, when it was too late, much too late.

She couldn't figure it out at first. She felt weak and light, as if she were floating. She could see and hear all the sirens and shouting voices, but they didn't seem to see or hear her. They were bent over the nearly nude body of a young woman lying on the worn carpet of a dirty, shoddy apartment. There was blood soaked into her blond hair, and her green eyes had a vacant glassy stare. She also saw a small, dark spot, no, it was a hole in the girl's temple.

Clothes lay scattered on the floor; they seemed to have been cut away for the paramedics to do their work. The clothes matched what she was wearing; wasn't that strange? They worked quickly, urgently but also impersonally, with no regard for her tattered dignity. One of them sadly shook his head, and the others stopped.

"She's all yours, Doug," the paramedic said sadly. "What a waste."

She looked down surprised because the body looked like her. Suddenly she felt a sharp pain, and then quickly remembered the glimpse of a gun, just the slightest image of it, and the explosion that she'd felt more than heard.

Slowly the realization came to her: This was her! She was dead. She had been shot and murdered. And she'd deserved it. She rebelled; no, she didn't deserve this. All she had done was take a small package from Miguel, which she was supposed to give to Jack, and take a package from him back to Miguel. But Jack had pulled a gun and shot her without hesitation. Then she remembered he'd done things to her, to the empty shell that had been her body, before the police came.

The paramedics left her body and the watching police officers began to examine the surrounding area, looking at every detail. The man who the paramedic had spoken to stood a small distance away, talking to one of the police officers before moving closer to examine the body. She watched as he knelt and examined the body and the area surrounding it.

She looked at him curiously, seeming slightly numb to her own predicament. The man named Doug was trim, somewhere close to fifty, with brown hair that had traces of silver, and very old, gray eyes. He was professional, almost dispassionate. She realized that this was just a job to him, but to her it was murder, her murder.

She knew she should have asked Miguel what was in the package, but she knew she wouldn't like the answer. So she'd hidden her head in the sand and done what Miguel asked. This was the fifth or sixth time she'd done the errand. Delivered drugs, she realized with the insight of the newly dead. She was going to have a hard time explaining that one to her father who was probably waiting for her somewhere, shaking his head sadly with that disappointed look she hadn't seen since he'd died of cancer two years earlier. She wanted to see him again but she wasn't looking forward to that look…

She was never sure why it happened; it wasn't anything she did, but she stayed with the man named Doug, the one she noticed looking over her body. She was somewhere nearby and heard him when he made that terrible phone call to her mother. She heard the polite, but dispassionate way he'd told her mother that she had been killed. She heard through the phone line her mother's wail of grief. She was there when her body was moved, wheeled out and finally put aside, in a cold dark place, waiting for the autopsy. She saw the man leave to go to another scene. There alone she waited; waited for what, she didn't know.

Suddenly it was the next day. She was watching as a group of friends met at a small apartment. It was cozy and filled with warmth. The group was lighthearted and smiling. Chatting over the latest gossip of the day, movies they been to and…

A man smiled at one of the women, "Have you seen my new paddle? He held it out to her. "Would you like to have me try it out on you?"

"Sure, later. I want to eat first." She hugged him briefly. "We'll play in a little while, okay?"

"Oh my God," she thought, "I'm at the munch, The Santa Del Rio Spanking munch!"

A man came out of the kitchen. "Hey there, sweetie." He hugged the woman warmly. "I'm glad you could make it."

If a spirit could have, she would have fainted. It was Doug. Of all the people in the world, she thought, I get a kinky coroner.

Alycia watched with amazement as the man who had presided

over her death scene joked and greeted people. It seemed they called him Ed, but she knew that wasn't his name. She learned why when he did a pretty good imitation of the famous talking horse. They were a group of obviously good friends. Then she watched as the man they called Ed welcomed a new person into the group with the same warmth and acceptance as he greeted everyone else. She heard varied and interesting conversations about everything except politics and the weather. She saw a nice looking man, younger than most who sat in the corner, chatting and relaxed, but he seemed sad and lonely somehow. She noticed that everyone seemed to feel at home and relaxed, even a young woman who was led into the bedroom by Ed who was laughing.

As the woman laid herself across the man's lap, she was smiling and joking. She continued to smile and joke even as she was spanked. Smile and joke, and gasp once in a while. The man stopped spanking her and picked out a paddle from a gym bag loaded with many various implements; Alycia was shocked. The paddle he picked was thick, dark wood, and the paddle surface looked to be about four by six inches, with a handle.

He cracked it down on the woman's bottom and she yelped and laughed. As the paddling continued, she yelped and squirmed. Her bottom turned darker pink, then red. She made an occasional quip, which seemed to encourage the paddler to swat her harder.

Once or twice she said, "Not so hard!"

And to Alycia's amazement, Ed's paddling eased up. Then he stopped and dug into the bag again.

Another couple came into the room, and the woman on the bed slid over obligingly. Soon another spanking was underway. The two women being spanked chatted with each other even as they were getting spanked. Ed came back with a leather strap and began to use it on Alycia; she tucked her head onto her arm, seemingly relaxed, and smiling softly as she was strapped.

Later Alycia saw other women and even men getting spanked. Ed himself took a long spanking that included the paddle, several straps and a pair of wooden spoons. He was the most bruised of any of the partygoers, and he clearly enjoyed every moment of it. Many times the spankings were harder than what the first woman received, but at no time did she see anyone ask someone to stop or even to ease up without that request being followed immediately. There was nothing that could be called abuse, but there were plenty of red bottoms, laughter and friendship.

As the party wound down, Alycia felt herself begin to fade. There was a voice inside her which seemed to communicate without words, with just feelings and symbols. She knew that she was being asked if she had learned anything, if she would do things differently if she could. She didn't know how to answer that voice if she had to say it, think it or just let herself feel, but her answer was "yes." She managed that thought, along with a wish that she would have that chance, even as she faded completely away from herself.

She was looking down at herself at the place where she'd died. It seemed to be the previous night. Her body was uncovered, and the official car from the coroner's office was just pulling up.

"Who declared this woman dead?" Doug asked sharply, all business. He was standing about twenty feet from her body, looking things over and speaking to the witnesses and policemen.

"The paramedics," a young police officer said, pointing out the paramedics who were just loading their medical equipment back into their truck.

"Well, tell them to do the job right next time," he said. "That woman is still alive."

Alycia lost all consciousness and sense of self. Then she felt as if time had passed, felt like herself, as if she had a body again. She muttered and looked up at the men standing over her. Doug was one of them.

"Ed," she whispered, labored and thready.

"What'd she say?" someone asked.

"She said Ed," another voice replied. "She must have seen the gun. Maybe there was someone else here and she tried to warn him or her."

She tried to focus on Ed's face. She was barely conscious. But she managed to whisper again. "No. You're Ed. Saved me."

Those were the last words she managed before losing consciousness. She awoke in the hospital.

It was two days later before she saw the man she knew as Ed again.

He couldn't resist coming to see her. Partially because it was a novelty for him to see someone alive and getting better after he'd been called to a scene, a pleasant novelty in this case. Also his curiosity was aroused; who was she and how did she know him? Ed knew, and liked, a lot of young women. He was no playboy, but he was told that he was a great friend. And, he thought to himself, a great playmate. He hardly ever forgot a face, but he couldn't remember Alycia. So who was she and how did they know each other? Laughing to himself he thought that maybe he'd remember her better if she turned over and bared her bottom, but even as he thought it, he decided it was better not to tell her that.

Alycia looked up from her bed and smiled as Ed entered her hospital room. "I was hoping I'd get to see you again. To thank you."

"I didn't do anything special, just saved myself some work," Ed grinned. "But I have one question. How do you know me? I'm sorry, but I can't remember you. Where have we met?"

"We haven't," Alycia grinned at his puzzled face. "Yet."

"Then how do you know me? And by my nickname?" he asked, confused. "Only a small group of people knows me by that name."

"You wouldn't believe me if I told you," Alycia muttered.

"But you will tell me," he prompted.

"Okay, but it's weird." Alycia drew a deep breath, gathered her nerves and began, blurting out her story in a rush before she could change her mind. "You see, I died in that shabby apartment. Really died. You were there and looked me over. I heard you call my mother to inform her of my death. Then things went black. The next thing I knew, I was sort of floating over the munch at your house, watching and listening. I remember thinking that if I'd had any sense, I'd be at that munch instead of lurking on the fringes of the Santa Del Rio Spanking list. I remember that I was sort of mad that I'd wasted my life. And I remember a feeling, more of a questioning, deep inside me asking if I'd learned anything, if I could change things with a second chance. I answered yes. Then I was back at the crime scene, you noticed me moving slightly, and I wound up here."

"Wow." Ed didn't know what else to say. He was at a very uncharacteristic loss for words. He paused a long moment and asked quietly, "What's next?"

"I've already made a deal to turn in Miguel and any of his friends who are involved with drugs. So I guess I'm off the hook, well, except for a few years probation." She swallowed hard. "Don't get me wrong, I'm glad I'm not going to prison but it seems wrong for me to go free, like I got away with something I shouldn't have."

"You did," Ed said firmly. "And it was a major screw-up. It could have cost you your life. Have you thought about how your mother would have felt? Heck, how about how she feels now, knowing the danger you were in, even when it turns out you're going to recover?"

"She's supportive, but she's also hurt and angry," Alycia said. "She tries to hide it, but I can tell."

"And you still feel guilty?" Ed prodded.

Alycia nodded, tears forming unexpectedly in her eyes.

"Is you father still alive?" Ed asked. When she shook her head, he continued, "Any brothers? Fiancée?"

"No," Alycia whispered. "There was Miguel but that's over."

"I'm glad to hear it," Ed said shortly. "But still there should be *someone...*"

"What for?" Alycia asked.

"To make sure you pay for this mistake and learn from it," Ed said grimly.

"Pay for it how?" Alycia asked.

"Someone should give you the thrashing you deserve," Ed stated flatly.

"Thrashing?" Alycia said alarmed.

"Yes. A good hard thrashing, to make sure you've learned your lesson, to make sure you never act so stupidly again with your life, and even," Ed paused, "even to relieve some of your guilt. You need to pay for your mistake and move on."

"Part of me agrees with you, and part of me is too scared to think about it," Alycia whispered. "I'm almost glad I don't have anybody to do it."

"Find someone, and ask him or her to do it," Ed advised. "Your guilt will eat you up inside until you do. This was the biggest screw up I can think of."

They sat and talked for a while, half-glancing at the TV set mounted on the hospital room wall.

Suddenly Alycia said in a small voice, "Ed, will you do it? You're the only one I know who knows anything about spanking."

"I do pleasure spankings, erotic and playful, where the spankee has a lot of control over how hard and long the spanking is," he said. "That's not what you need; you need a real spanking, what's called a punishment spanking. Long and hard and painful, and totally out of your hands." He paced around the room. "When are you getting out of here?"

"Tomorrow," Alycia said.

"That's Monday," Ed said, thinking out loud. "And when do you go back to work?"

"Probably next Monday."

"Tell you what: I'll give you my number," Ed said. "You think about it, and call me. If you really want me to do it, and remember, it's gonna hurt like the devil, call me Thursday and I'll do it on Friday. That would give you the weekend to recover before you return to work."

"Recover?" Alycia whispered.

"Yes." Ed was firm, "If you want to do the right thing and take` your punishment, you will need time to recover. And Alycia, you will have to call me Thursday and ask me to come over and punish you, and spell out exactly what you need; you will need to ask me to make sure it really hurts."

"I have to do all that? But it's… " Alycia trailed off.

"Part of your punishment," Ed said without mercy. "You must ask for the spanking and you must submit to it, the best you can. However long and hard it is, and whatever I use. It won't be easy."

"Use?" she almost whimpered.

"You know, a paddle, a leather strap, a hairbrush, a cane, probably all those," Ed grinned grimly. "Lucky for you, I already have lots of toys."

"Oh, your toys," Alycia gulped. "How lucky."

"I'll leave now. Call me." He leaned over and kissed her forehead gently. "If you dare."

"Goodbye, Ed."

He waited for her call, almost as nervous as he imagined Alycia to be. He liked spanking and getting spanked by women, but this would be different. He knew he could do it, but it had been a long time since he'd spanked a woman to tears.

Alycia called. "Ed, this is Alycia. I know I need to be punished. Would you please come over tomorrow and spank me?"

"Do you need a hard spanking?" Ed asked.

"Yes," she answered. "Very hard."

"On your bare bottom?" he prompted.

"What?" she shrieked. He merely waited. "Yes," she finally answered.

"With whatever paddles or implements I feel like using?"

"Yes."

"Then put it all together and ask me nicely," he instructed.

"Ed, would you please come over tomorrow and give me a hard spanking, on my bare bottom, with whatever implements you feel would be appropriate?" she whispered.

"Yes, Alycia," he answered cheerfully, "I'd be glad to. I'll be there at eight PM. Please be ready. And Alycia, no drugs or alcohol before or after, nothing to calm your nerves or dull the pain, understand?"

"Yes, Ed," she whispered, her voice shaky.

"And Alycia, for now the correct answer is yes, sir." Ed knew he was rubbing it in.

"Yes, sir." She sounded meek.

He hung up. Then he dug through his toys, selecting the best ones for use on Alycia. A large wooden paddle was discarded for one that was just a bit smaller, but the wood was thicker; the leather strap was long and thick, but pliable; the hairbrush was wooden with an oval back; and the cane was whippy and flexible. He put those four in a small duffel bag.

He arrived promptly at eight. He knocked on the door and she let him in, going pale at the sight of his duffel bag full of toys. He hugged her for a minute and then said gently, "Go over to the corner, raise up that skirt, lower your panties down to your knees so that your bottom is exposed, and face the corner until I tell you to move."

Alycia was visibly shaken but she obeyed without a word.

Ed sat there for a few minutes, gathering his strength for the task ahead. He was a spanker, but he was not someone who liked causing real pain. His spankings were intended to give pleasure. He did, however, recognize that she needed this punishment both to remind herself of the consequences of reckless behavior, and in order to forgive herself. After only a few minutes, he pulled a straight-backed chair into the center of the room.

"Come here, Alycia, over my knees," he said firmly.

The wait had been only a few minutes but it seemed like forever to Alycia. And still it seemed too short; she wasn't ready yet. With her panties still around her knees, she moved over to the chair and gingerly placed herself in position over Ed's knees.

He began spanking her without the gradual warm up he was used to giving his partners when he played. SLAP! SLAP! SLAP! The spanking was hard but not especially severe. Alycia squirmed but remained silent other than a gasp or two. He speeded up and she yelped, squirming even harder. She began to put one hand back to cover her tender behind.

"Don't even think of trying to cover your bottom," Ed said very forcefully, "or I'll be forced to start all over again."

Alycia moved her hand quickly and forced herself to submit. It hurt much worse than she expected. What she failed to realize was that Ed had held back just a little. Not that he was showing her mercy, but he had a lot more planned and he wanted to pace it, just a bit.

He stopped spanking her after about a hundred spanks and told her to go back to the corner. He ordered her to keep her skirt raised and the panties around her knees. She stood there, tears forming in her eyes, but not really crying, not yet.

She started to reach back to rub her bottom but the Ed said sternly, "No rubbing, ever, or we start over."

She quickly moved her hands, putting them where Ed told her to, on top of her head. Her skirt was tucked up against the wall in front of her. Her bottom was warm and throbbing, beautifully colored; not red but past pink. She knew the ordeal was just beginning. She sniffed loudly and stood there.

Ed gave her another order. "Take your skirt off completely, pick my paddle off the table and bring it to me, then get back into position over my knees. Now!"

She slowly followed his instructions. Her eyes were downcast, as if she were searching the carpet for something she'd dropped. She handed him the paddle without a word and draped herself back over his knees.

"I'm giving you fifty with the paddle because you risked losing at least fifty years off your life," he said firmly. "Count each one and thank me for it."

"Fifty? You've got to be kidding!" she protested.

"We could double that if it's not enough," he said mildly.

"No, fifty's okay," she said softly.

"And remember, I said count," he reminded her.

"What?" She was surprised.

"You know, say: One, thank you, sir, Two, thank you, sir," he explained." If you lose count, we start over; if you miss a number, we repeat that stroke."

"But that's humiliating!" she protested.

"Exactly!" Was his only reply. "Are you ready?"

There was no answer. "The only acceptable answer is an enthusiastic: Yes, sir!" he prodded. "Are you ready?"

"Yes, sir," she replied weakly.

"Didn't seem very enthusiastic to me, but it'll do." He brought the paddle down with a quick hard SMACK!

"One, thank you, sir," she managed, but the pain was much worse than the hand spanking.

The blows came quickly with only a slight pause between them, just enough for her to get the words out. In fact, on a couple of the blows she didn't get the words out fast enough and he repeated those blows. Alycia really tried to say the hateful phrase as quickly as possible.

At twenty-five, he paused and stroked her behind gently for a short time, before continuing ever harder. Alycia began to protest until she found out that protesting interfered with her count and added to her punishment. At fifty, she was limp and crying silently. The urge to rub was almost irresistible.

"Now, go put the paddle back where you found it, get the strap and bring it to me," he said coldly, fighting his natural sense of compassion. "Then bend over the arm of the sofa and stay in position while I give you fifty with the strap."

"No! Not more, I've had enough!" she cried out.

"If this was a fun spanking or an erotic spanking, I'd stop when you said to," Ed said firmly. "But this is discipline, real punishment, and punishment for the worst thing a person could possibly do: You committed a crime, carrying drugs, and that was bad enough. You aided and abetted your lousy boyfriend in the drug trade because he was too smart to get himself caught with the stuff, and that's worse, but worst of all, you let yourself get killed for something that you could have avoided. So bend over, count the strokes out loud; count and say thank you after each one. If you move or try to cover your bottom you'll get ten extra strokes. So hold still and endure. Do you understand?"

"Yes, Ed," she whimpered. "I'll do my best."

"I know you will," he said grimly, steeling himself for the task ahead.

He swung the strap fast and hard. It landed with a loud CRACK on her already tender, aching bottom. She screamed and jumped before counting the stroke.

CRACK! CRACK! CRACK!

"My God! That hurts!" she shrieked.

"It's supposed to," he told her without a hint of mercy, even though he felt it. "Keep your count and your thank you's coming, hold your position, and do not reach back to protect your bottom so we can get this over with as soon as possible."

She tried, really tried but she didn't quite make it. At the fortieth stroke she raised up and put her hands over her throbbing bottom.

He reacted instantly. "That's another ten! Get back in position now or it's another twenty!"

Somehow, finding a reserve of strength and courage she never realized she had, she made it without any further problems.

"Stand up, put the strap back where you found it, and go to the corner; stand there with your bottom facing me with your hands on your head," he said without any emotion. "And no rubbing or the strapping will be repeated."

"Oh God, no!" she said fervently. "I'll do exactly what you say."

"And shut up, do it quietly," Ed instructed. "I want you to think about how you got yourself into this mess. I know the obvious thing to do is blame Miguel, and he is a louse, but you are responsible for your own actions and decisions. Think about it." He left her there for a full half-hour. Her arms were aching by the time he returned, but she didn't dare lower them.

"All right, we're almost done," Ed said almost cheerfully. "Fetch the hairbrush and assume the position across my knees for fifty with the brush."

"And that's all?" she asked hopefully.

"Not quite." That sounded ominous. "Come here quickly. Now, or it'll be sixty."

She was over his knees in a flash; reluctantly, but in a flash.

WHAP! WHAP! WHAP!

The brush landed with a stunning regularity but without the extreme severity of the strap. He didn't need to be so severe; she was badly hurt already, her bottom was fiery red with purple blotches and stripes from the paddle and strap. The brush merely forced her to endure and submit. She cried openly throughout the whole paddling, but she never squirmed or protested.

"Put the brush back and bring me the cane. Assume the position you used for the strap," Ed told her calmly. "Only ten strokes with the cane."

"Only ten?" she asked cautiously.

"Trust me, ten will be more than enough," Ed said tightly. "And for every moment you delay, I'll add more on."

She handed him the cane and got into position quickly. She stood there shivering and afraid.

"Now if you hold position and count for me, it'll be over in less than a minute, however if you do not... " he trailed off.

"I'll do my best, sir," she whispered.

THWACK! THWACK! THWACK! They were very harsh cuts with the cane. Ed barely avoided drawing blood, and that was partially because he aimed lower, for the crease between her buttocks and thighs and her upper thighs. THWACK! THWACK! THWACK! She counted in a hoarse whisper, but it was audible. THWACK! THWACK! She jumped but got back into position very quickly.

"Sorry, sir. Eight, sir," she whispered. "Thank you, sir."

"That's okay, my dear," he said gently. "You're almost done."

THWACK! THWACK!

"That's it girl, you're done. Into the corner with you," Ed said, relieved himself.

She stood in the corner, crying and shaking. The need to rub her sore bottom was excruciating, but she didn't touch it. Ed picked up his implements and wiped each one carefully with an antiseptic wipe before putting it back into his bag. He pulled a small bottle out the bag, and wandered into her kitchen. He explored a bit and found just what he wanted. First, he put some cool water on a cloth, scooped a few of her ice cubes into small bowl, and poured two glasses of wine.

"Here, my dear." He handed her the glass of wine, then very gently and carefully wiped off her bottom with the cool, damp cloth. He rubbed an ice cube over the reddest areas. He wiped off most of the moisture and gently rubbed her bruises with Arnica.

He took her hand gently and led her to the sofa. They sat down and he pulled her gently onto his lap. He folded his arms around her and drew her head to lean on his chest. He just let her cry. He whispered soft and gentle words of comfort into her ear and gently stroked her back. When her sobbing stopped, he let her up.

"Did you learn something?" he asked gently.

"Yes, I sure did," she answered. "I've learned to value my life and enjoy myself. I've learned that it's never too late to try new things, as long as you are alive. I've also learned to watch out for the consequences of my actions, and… " She slanted a glance at him, almost grinning.

"And?"

"And to be careful who you ask, when you need a punishment spanking," she said with a trace of defiance.

"Good idea," Ed grinned. "And you will come to the munch in two weeks? Or I'll be back here, and you do not want that. Do you understand?"

"Not really. Why do I have to come to the munch?" She was puzzled.

"Because then you can find out how a play spanking feels." He paused, and continued with a devilish gleam in his eyes, "And you can try spanking me!"

"Oh, I see. In that case, I'll be there all right." She laughed as he walked over to the door. "I can get revenge."

He kissed her gently on the forehead and left. Over the next few days he called her three times. Each time he asked how she was and talked casually for a few minutes before telling her to call him if she needed a friend. Two weeks later he called her and reminded her to come to the munch.

She walked into the munch a little nervous. She vaguely wondered if he had said anything about her to any of the other members, but once she thought about it she knew he hadn't. He greeted her like any new guest, without a word or gesture to acknowledge he'd ever seen her before. She felt at home, welcomed and accepted. She found herself sitting next to the younger guy, the lonely looking one she'd noticed when she visited as a spirit.

He looked over at her and said softly, "Hi, I'm Dean. I know you're new here but would you like to play?"

She was scared; her only spanking had been the very severe one she'd received from Ed, but somehow she gathered the courage to answer him with a soft but firm, "Yes, I'd like that. But please, go easy on me, I'm new to this."

"Just tell me if I do anything you don't like or if you want me to go easier," he said with a tender smile. "I'm only here to please you."

Ed was off to the side of the room talking to a woman who wanted to paddle him very hard, just for the fun of it. With a warm smile on his face he watched the younger couple walk over to the bed and begin to play. He knew what would happen just as well as if he'd seen it before, and he was right.

Within moments she knew the difference between discipline and play. She also knew that the lonely guy would not be lonely any longer.

This one is a tribute to many dear friends, in two main groups. They will know who they are. I wonder if they know what they mean to me. I value them as friends and fellow spankos. They are generous, decent and caring, the best people I know.

Eleven

She's No Angel

I wrote this thinking of a few discussions we've had over the years, about how we can be spankos and still believe in God and Christ. This is my attempt to put my answer to some of those questions in a story, with a little humor and a lot of love.

I am no theologian, but I do believe in God. I believe He has warmth, humor and whimsy. He created panda bears, koalas, zebras and armadillos didn't he? And a bug called a walking stick. Now if that isn't humor, what is? Could a random universe be filled with that much wonder and joy? This one takes a while to get to the spanking but I hope you think it's worth the journey.

She had always been a brat, all her life, so why should it be any different now that she was dead? She was still herself.

Imagine it though, she was an angel. She thought, wasn't that a kick in the as... er, head? How could a brat be an angel? She'd ruin her reputation. Well, to be truthful, she never was a malicious brat, and she sure wasn't spoiled. She never lied, stole or deliberately hurt anybody. She was just a prankster, a smart mouth and a bottom.

Still, some of the more senior angels wondered why she was there. To be sure, they never really *questioned;* it must be part of the plan. The Maker always had a plan, but they did wonder.

She just didn't seem to fit in. For one thing, she was just too happy. While they were filled with perfect joy, she was filled with the joy of life. They were pious and somber, content in their prayers. She was smiling and laughing, and eager to explore and learn. They loved each other as fellow angels, but she made friends. Still, she had her good traits, they readily admitted.

She had a really generous heart filled with love for her fellow man, and most especially filled with love for The Maker. She had a mouth on her though; she was always ready with a joke, a light comment or quip, and some of them were quite irreverent. And she was always filled with good cheer, but some thought too much good cheer. The girl giggled and gushed. She practically bubbled over with fun.

The rest of the angels were happy, of course, they were in Heaven, so how could they help it? But they muted their joy with somber piety, proper behavior and long, solemn faces. They were reverent, while she was irreverent.

Their reaction to the girl was almost the same reaction they had when the first few rock and roll musicians went up there. Admittedly, rock and roll musicians who made it there were still few and far between. Most of them went somewhere else. Still, some did arrive in heaven and they joined the heavenly chorus and band, but they were greeted with censure and frowns.

They interrupted the organ music, the string quartets and the harps with *that* sound. Never you mind that Psalm 150 said to praise Him with stringed instruments, loud cymbals, trumpets and dance. And that Psalm 98 said to make a joyful noise, a loud noise. It didn't mean rock, even Christian rock. Of course not. It meant a sedate and somber peaceful joyful noise.

Luckily, the senior angels soon learned that The Maker and his Son liked the raucous music if it were played from a loving, decent heart. As usual, they judged what was in the soul, not outward trappings.

So it was with her. The outward trappings were her manner, her dress and of course, the spanking games she had played in life. Her soul and mind were filled with love of life and of The Maker. She helped others when she could, with no thought of self or reward, either on earth or in Heaven. She gave of herself freely.

She didn't preach, but she never hid her beliefs either, and because of that she reached some members of a group that was focused on more earthy delights, and without words showed them that there was more to life, and that they could enjoy it all without giving up their fun.

Her death was a bummer, she had to admit. She was driving home one night after a party, and her car was hit out of nowhere by a drunk driver. She died instantly. The other driver walked away with minor injuries. Her blood was analyzed but no traces of alcohol or any drugs were found. His was double the legal limit for intoxication, and that was only the alcohol; they never bothered to find out what other chemicals he might have had.

At the scene, even as she realized she was dead, she prayed for the other driver to be all right. She prayed for him to stop drinking. She did not pray for him to get off easy; that she refused to do. If he got off easy, he could do this again that much sooner: Drive drunk and kill another innocent victim. She forgave him for killing her, but she wanted him jailed to save others. The instant and instinctive prayer for the man who killed her was part of the reason she found herself in with the good guys.

The senior angels got together and talked about her; not that they were judging her, you understand. They had been warned about that many times. They were just concerned that she might be a bad influence and disruptive. The most senior angel pondered if she were truly ready for heaven. You see, The Maker had a plan for everyone. A divine plan. He guarded and watched over all His children. In His plan, some thought to themselves, there was a flaw. Well, not a flaw, His plan was perfect, but there was an anomaly. He knew what they thought of course, He always knew, but human nature was still human nature, even in heaven. What the senior angels thought was a flaw was really a considered and brilliant part of His plan: He left room for free will.

It was free will that killed her. Free will let the man drink and drive. Free will even put her in a car that night. Her free will did nothing wrong; the other man's free will killed her.

There was another angel in heaven, a very junior angel, who had known her in life. It was thought for a moment, or maybe a decade, by some that he was to be her soul mate, but he developed a rare childhood cancer and entered heaven at the age of 15. No one except The Maker knew if these early deaths were part of His plan, were random, or a result of free will on a level they could not begin to comprehend. They discussed it and concluded that even they did not know, and could never know the scope of His plan. They just had to accept and believe, as they had to on earth.

Because of his youth and his illness, he had never become very worldly, never grown to manhood. He had faced his disease with courage and dignity beyond his years, but he never faced the humdrum world of job hunting or college exams, never knew the joy of human love, marriage and babies. Sometimes it's easier to be courageous during a crisis than it is just to live a good, decent life. They knew that while he was accepting of his fate, he secretly felt cheated. That happened sometimes, even with older humans who entered heaven. A man of ninety might feel the same way. Usually the older souls who felt that way had wasted their own lives. This boy had not.

He had asked The Maker for more time, wording his request as a way to be a better angel. The Maker heard many such requests, and usually found no reason to veer from His plan. As He looked in this boy's heart He saw that the request was sincere and true. This boy was an extraordinary soul, and with some more seasoning, more experience, he would be a mighty influence on earth and go on to become an extraordinary angel.

He pondered. Even the Almighty ponders. He looked at His original plans for the boy and realized that the new young angel, the one who arrived by way of the drunken driver had, in fact, been destined to be this boy's soul mate. The senior angels felt that she too, needed some experience, some maturity, some, well, seasoning to be her most effective. He sent for the senior angel.

"I want these two to meet and talk," He told the angel. "There is much they can do to help each other. These two together can be far more than the sum of their parts."

"Yes, Lord," the angel replied. "Thy will be done."

The senior angel told the young angel to go and talk with her.

There were no other remarks, no instructions. Just go and talk.

The young angel went to her and introduced himself. "I am Seth," he said softly. "I knew you on earth."

"Hi, I'm Angela, ironic name huh?" she replied with a pert grin. "I'm sorry I don't remember you, but it's a pleasure to meet you."

"I was in your junior high school and I would have been in high school with you but I got so sick; I never had a chance to go," he said softly. "And as I remember, I wanted to go to high school. I think I would have asked you out."

"I wondered why I never had a decent boyfriend in high school," she thought for a moment, and then a smile broke over her face. "I remember! You look so different now, so healthy. We never saw you that way, not once you got sick. We all wondered how you were, and we sent cards and notes to you. We prayed, too. Did you ever know?"

"Yes, I did," Seth smiled back. "You gave me courage and hope."

"That was all we could do, although we wanted to do more," Angela said remembering. "We also sent notes and letters to your parents after you died."

"Well, it was a downer to die at fifteen, let me tell you," he said smiling. "I never got to ask you out. I never had a chance to go to college, get married or have a family. And," his voice dropped, "what a let down to die a virgin."

"He'll hear!" she said with a squeak.

"He knows all our thoughts," the boy said. "He heard it before I said it. He loves me as I am. Now if the senior angel had heard… "

"Trouble?" she winked.

"Big time," he winked back.

"Well," she said, "I made it to the ripe old age of twenty-four. I went to college and found a great job, and I still died a virgin."

"As I recall, no one was a virgin at twenty-four." He was surprised.

"Well, you can't possibly know how many people that fact would shock. Here, maybe not, but on earth… " She paused

139

wrinkling up her nose. "It's just that I believed that sex should wait for marriage. I stuck to that belief. I dated quite often and I came close a few times, but it wasn't right somehow. I did play however."

"Play?" he asked. "What do you mean?"

"Well, He already knows so I might as well say," she said, although she looked over her shoulder for the senior angel. "I played spanking games. I was a spanko. I was also a brat, a bottom."

"What?" Seth was shocked. "I didn't know they let you guys in up here. Not that I'm judging you, I mean. It's just that this is a pretty staid crowd. Prim and proper, you know."

"Well, as I've said, we didn't have sex. We just played. I always felt it was good clean fun, but there were a few debates over the years." She smiled at the memory of her earthly friends. "I guess I was on the winning side. Anyway, that's in the past. I do have a question about things here though."

"What is it?" Seth was still reeling from her revelations.

"Why aren't there any children here?" She was puzzled. "I know far too many children die young. Yet, you're the youngest person, er angel, I've met."

"Some of the children are here. It's just that they are as they would be as adults," Seth explained. "And some have been given a second chance at life."

"What do you mean?" she wondered.

"They are reborn either to the same family, as another child, or," he paused, "if their parents were bad, they were given to a new family."

"So that's why there are no children?" she puzzled aloud. "I wondered why they seemed to have such a hard time accepting me. I thought there would be lots of children full of laughter and fun but there are none, and the senior angels don't seem to have any sense of humor."

"Too true, they need to be around children," Seth said. "Some of them have forgotten to have fun mixed in with their perfect joy."

"Then why are you here?" she asked. "As a teenager, not an adult. And you have obviously not been reborn. Why is that?"

"I do not know." He shook his head. "But there is a reason. Always."

That was the start of many days of laughter, teasing and long talks. They grew close together.

She had other friends too; she saw a few friends she knew from her earthly life, and her relations: her grandmother and an aunt. Her parents were still on earth, and it troubled her that they were grieving. She wanted to comfort them.

She knew some of her friends from the spanko group had visited them, offering friendship and comfort along with uneasy explanations of how they knew her. She even learned that the man who killed her had gone to prison and was getting counseling behind bars. She prayed for him.

She wanted to play with Seth but one of her friends from the spanko group who got to heaven before she had, told her it would not work. There was no hitting in heaven, of any kind. Not even playful spankings. He sighed with the memory of how he used to spank her.

The Maker came to a decision. Angela was called to the senior angel and sent back to earth. In the blink of an eye without any warning, she found herself in a hospital bed, coming out of a coma. She was alive and everything was fine. It seemed she had never died. She'd just been in a coma.

If she told anyone about being in heaven, they told her all her experiences were delusions or drug induced dreams. Maybe it was one of those near death experiences? She knew in her heart they were wrong, but she also realized that she had been given a gift by The Maker. She stopped telling anyone about it. She kept her mouth shut and concentrated on her recovery. She did miss Seth, though.

Then one day she saw him and knew him instantly. He was an intern. He was a bit older than he was in heaven, about her age, and working on his neurological rotation.

He knew her from somewhere but could not remember where

or how they had met. She told him how she'd known him from school but omitted meeting him in heaven. She had already learned that any talk of heaven would be met with skepticism. She guessed too much talk about having died and been to heaven might even earn her a padded room.

There was an instant chemistry between the two of them. They talked a lot. One day he told her about having cancer as a child. His family had moved out of state to be near a famous treatment center and prayed for a miracle. It had worked. He got a miracle – he was cured.

As they talked, he realized that they had met in junior high school. It was shortly before his family had moved across the country for his treatment.

They were together constantly. She knew he was meant for her, that much she remembered. She also knew that they had been together in heaven, and they had only been given a short time for this second chance on earth; about seventy years to live and love and grow together.

They took advantage of the new life they had been given. They began dating when she was out of the hospital. They went to dinner, movies, concerts and plays. He soon learned that she loved riding horses, so he learned to ride. She learned he loved football, so she learned more about the game and watched with him. Angela had often missed church before she died, but now it seemed more important, more vital. They went to church together. They planned to marry in a few months.

One day she told him about spanking and how she missed playing. It happened because she got calls and emails from the group. He wondered who these people were, especially the men. He wasn't jealous, he told himself, just curious.

"I've been meaning to talk to you about that," she said with a blush. "These are my friends from a spanking group. We play spanking games. It's good clean fun. I'd like you to come with me to a party and meet these friends. I've missed them."

"Isn't my company good enough for you?" Seth puzzled.

"I love your company but I miss the friendship I've gotten

from this group?" Angela said softly. "Please come to a party with me?"

"What would I have to do?" he asked.

"Just talk, visit and get to know people," she said. "You may see and hear a few things but you don't have to participate in any way unless you want to. There is no sex of course, just play."

"And what about you?" he prodded.

"Of course I won't play unless you feel comfortable about it," she said firmly. "I miss playing but the way I feel is that you are more important; too important for me to go against your wishes in this matter."

They went to a party together. He was surprised at how much he liked the members of the group. They were open, accepting and welcomed him without question. No one even seemed to notice that he didn't play. Although she had been out of the hospital for quite a while and was fully recovered, they were so concerned about Angela's health that they were more than content to just visit with her.

Seth saw and heard spankings; they would be impossible to miss.

They talked after the party. He enjoyed meeting the group and liked the people. He even admitted he was tempted to play. He did question if spanking was a sin though.

"I just don't want anything to stop us from being together, either here or in heaven," was the way he phrased it.

"I already made it to heaven once," she told him. "And I was already a spanko."

For the first time, she told him everything she remembered about her death and heaven.

"It sounds like a near death experience," he said quietly. "And those aren't proven to be accurate."

"No." She was firm. "I've read up on it, and near death experiences are about seeing things you couldn't see, like the bald spot on the top of your doctor's head because you were floating above him. Or seeing and hearing what your friends say in the hallway outside your room. And there's the famous white light, with those you've loved and lost waiting for you. This wasn't that."

"Then what was it?" he wondered aloud.

"I spent time in heaven. I can't say how long because time is different there. But I saw angels; met with them and talked with them, many times over a long period." She paused. "The senior angels were slightly disapproving. They seemed to feel I was too full of life, too energetic for heaven. They introduced me to a boy from my past who had died at the age of fifteen from cancer. He was to have been my soul mate. We talked many times. Even there in heaven, we fell in love."

She walked around the room, thinking. She decided to just say it outright. "It was you. Seth, we were given a second chance together and I would not endanger that for anything. If I thought for one second we would have to give up spanking I would, but we don't."

"Are you sure?" he asked quietly.

"Yes," she answered simply. "Oh yes. It was real."

"Then come here." He pulled her over his knees.

It was the first of many spankings, awkward and fumbling, but filled with fun and laughter. He soon learned how to please her, learned that she loved tickling almost as much as spanking. She soon learned to top him. They attended the parties as often as they could and participated fully.

Their wedding took place in the spring, in church, with the reception in a nearby banquet hall that boasted a beautiful garden. Their minister gladly officiated and their friends, all their friends, were there. The spankos were welcomed by everyone, although no one knew quite where they had met Seth or Angela.

On the ride from the church to the banquet hall, they put the security glass up to block the limo driver from seeing or hearing, and Seth gave Angela a very hard spanking, flipping up layers of petticoats, satin and lace, and lowering her lacy panties. It was hard, with yards of material to contend with, but it was fun. Jerry, the driver, was a spanko. He knew very well what was happening behind the glass, and he knew very well not to get to the reception too soon. He took the long way there.

They partied at the reception. They hugged and kissed everyone, laughed at raucous jokes and ribald remarks, and danced. They feasted on the catered buffet and tossed her bouquet and garter. Then they changed into traveling clothes, jumped in the limo and left.

They had a short flight to a local resort. It didn't matter where they went or what there was to do there since they expected to spend most of the honeymoon indoors. And they were right. They had both kept their chastity into their mid-twenties; it was enough. There was no more reason to delay, and no hesitation. There was only overwhelming passion and love.

He asked her if she wanted some privacy to prepare herself, perhaps thinking of the old movies where the bride spends an hour primping and putting on some lacy gown before joining her husband for a wedding night.

"Heck no," she laughed, as she stepped out of her high heels. "I'm as prepared as I'll ever be. Get over here, groom, and help me out of this dress!"

The clingy dress had no zipper. He gathered the material to peel it over her head, gradually raising it to expose her satin skin inch by gorgeous inch. He soon discovered the remaining lacy garter belt and lace topped stockings. There was also a tiny lacy pink thong. As he uncovered more of his bride, he saw the matching bra covering her generous breasts.

Once he lifted the dress over her head, she reached out and removed his tie. She began to unbutton his shirt. As he dropped the dress to the floor, she stripped off his shirt and pulled his undershirt over his head, running her hands softly over his muscled chest, reveling in the light covering of soft fur.

With a wide grin, she unfastened his belt. "Nice heavy, leather belt," she murmured. "We can play with this later."

He sat down for a moment to deal with his shoes, then stood and let her unbutton and unzip his pants. She worked the pants down his legs, and then he stepped out of them.

"My turn," he said, turning his attention to her garter belt and hose.

He reached up and worked at the front closure to her bra, but she was impatient and worked the clasp herself. They stood there, both with only their underwear on. Suddenly she laughed.

"What?" he asked.

"The only thing we're still wearing is our underwear, and we've already had that part of our clothes off, many times."

"Yeah," he grinned, "but only from the backside."

She turned down the bed covers and they both fell onto the bed. They made love with a passion and tenderness that more than made up for the waiting. It was glorious! They made love morning and night, and sometimes in between during that long week. Love that was passionate and fun.

It was well into the second day before the lovemaking was combined with a long delicious spanking. They were getting ready to go out and eat when he found some supposed fault with her, and pulled her over his knees. He spanked her for a long time after a good long warm up. His hand cracked down on her bare buttocks repeatedly, getting harder and faster until she thought she would have to tell him it was too hard. Then he stopped, and began stroking and tickling her all over her red bottom and along the length of her legs.

He picked her up and tossed her gently on the bed and told her to lie face down. He found his belt and whipped her with it; not too hard, but for a long time. Then he tickled her again, and this time he spent a long time at it. He rubbed cool lotion on her bottom and leaned over to nip the dark pink, warm flesh. His fingers slipped down to tease her, and the spanking play turned to passion. It was a long time before they had dinner, and then it was room service.

Before the honeymoon was over she was pregnant, although it was weeks before they learned of it. So they settled down with everyday jobs and friends, good times and bad, and a baby on the way. Their life as a married couple began.

And how did they fare?

They still play both spank and tickle, and they love. My God, how they love.

They both work hard to become better people. They are always ready to help others, to minister to their needs and counsel their souls. He often traveled to poor countries to help those without decent medical care, and she went along to help. And almost to her surprise, found that she could guide people spiritually.

Few people outside a very close circle of friends knew they were spankos. They never lost their love for life or each other.

The day she gave birth to her first child, The Maker looked down and smiled. He turned to His Son and said, "I just love a happy ending."

I expect to get blasted for this story; either it's too preachy or too sinful. If I get blasted by both sides equally I'll be happy, but there's the rub, as they say, because the people who think it's too sinful should not be reading this book, now should they?

Twelve

C. O. P. S.: Count On Painful Smacks

What might it be like if you could get paddled for traffic fines? What if you got a tough judge?

To say it seems strange now to think back on it is an understatement. It seems completely unbelievable. People thought it was something that could never happen, not here, not in modern America. Never. Especially not in a fairly small, rural town in northern California. But it did. A town reverted back to the Middle Ages, punishing its citizens for small violations with court ordered paddlings. It started because of the economy, like most things do, even if most people never think about it that way.

The city was in a terrible financial crisis. Surrounding farms were being foreclosed, young people were leaving for jobs in larger cities, and there was a stagnant economy. Less revenue was going into the city's coffers from taxes. There was little industry to speak of, and what there was made little money. There was almost no tourism. The city needed to raise money disparately. It was a sticky problem.

Some bright-eyed politician came up with a plan. What plan? Better financial management? No! It was never even mentioned. Foregoing the planned raises to self-important city officials? Never! Are you joking?

The actual city workers, of course, were told that their raises were put on hold. The street sweepers, garbage men, the police officers, secretaries, and even the teachers were told they had to wait indefinitely for a raise. That little announcement put the unions in an uproar and began a series of lawsuits that promised to generate some very expensive litigation.

The mayor and the city council members, along with the city attorney and the head financial planner however, all got their raises right on time, and bigger raises than most people realized…

Now all these city officials had to do was put their plan into effect.

What followed was one of those total disasters that happen when a well meaning, albeit self-serving official, puts his plans into effect without any thought or logic put into it. It backfired completely. In an attempt to raise more money, the city raised the fines on traffic tickets as high as they could. Speed traps were set up everywhere. The cops were very clever and very relentless, and they were unavoidable.

Everyone was getting caught. People who had never dreamed they could wind up in jail chose to do time instead of paying the fines because they simply could not afford to pay. The jails were full with so many people that the already grossly overcrowded system was strained to the breaking point. There were riots in the jails; not the prisons full of the hardened criminals, but the city jails full of traffic violators. People were missing too much time at work because of jail sentences. Businesses had trouble serving their customers because of missing employees. In fact, the businesses actually had fewer customers to serve.

Of course everyone complained about the situation. It was decided that an alternative to the harsh fines or the jail time should be found. Heaven forbid that they simply lower the fines to what they had been previously.

No, the fools worked hard until they came up with an even worse idea. They decided on corporal punishment, in the form of public paddling for traffic tickets, unless the violator could pay the exorbitant fine or afford to spend two months sitting in jail. Later, no city officials would admit to suggesting the court ordered paddlings.

The paddlings were actually done with a leather paddle. The outlandish idea was decried by everyone concerned with the judicial system. It was called cruel and barbaric. Judges, lawyers, the poor traffic violators and even police officers spoke out against it. There were some police officers, ones who would later volunteer to administer the punishment, who fought the plan a little less vigorously than everyone else. Some of them secretly smiled at the idea.

No one really knew why or how the plan wound up being put into effect. All anyone knew was that unfortunately, there were still three years remaining before the next city elections. Soon, recall petitions were being circulated. Lawsuits were filed challenging the plan's legality. Protesters marched in front of the courthouse. Reporters and the media were camped out in the few small motels. Their presence finally provided one of the few boons to the town's economy.

No one was paddled who hadn't been given an alternative, so officially no one was paddled against his or her will. It was just that the choice was so disproportionate that most people made the painful choice. A typical sentence would be: $1000.00, 60 days or 60 blows with a paddle. The paddling was officially called PHYSICAL CHASTISEMENT. This penalty was imposed for going as little as 5 miles over the speed limit, although officially it appeared on the record as 10.

It all backfired of course; the higher the fines, the more people submitted to the paddle, and the less money the city raised.

If anyone chose the alternative of being paddled, the court appointed doctor gave the person a quick exam. Just to see if he thought that the violator was physically fit for the punishment. The violator was then given an appointment for a date and time to report to the local police station for the paddling. It was very efficient and very quick, but of course it was not very painless, not painless at all!

Diana stood shaking in front of the judge. Although she was trying to remain composed, she was scared and embarrassed. And angry. She had not been speeding. She knew she was driving within two or three miles of the speed limit. She refused to believe it was any faster.

She was seething as she listened to the stern-faced judge when he made his pronouncement. "I find you guilty of speeding. You have a choice of paying a fine of $1000.00, spending 60 days in the city jail or corporal punishment with a paddle, 60 swats. Which is it to be?"

She had no choice, not really.

At first, when she was supposed to reply, she couldn't answer. She tried to speak but no sound came out. Finally, after a long pause she managed to mutter the dreaded words.

"Physical chastisement." In a small voice she said, "I'll take the 60 swats, your honor."

"Go next door, get your instructions as to time and place from the clerk and follow them to the letter. Any deviation will cost you more swats," the judge said. "I trust you can read instructions better than you can read speed limit signs?" he sneered at her.

"Yes, your honor." Her meek tone was a sham; she was furious. She went through the designated door.

In the small exam room next to the courtroom, she was given a very quick, superficial examination by a very impersonal male doctor. He listened to her heart and took her blood pressure. He told her to drop her slacks, and then asked her to bend over and grab her ankles.

Her face felt as if it was on fire as she complied with his instructions. The doctor felt her back and spine, then lowered her panties and spent quite a long time running his hands over her buttocks.

Then he asked her a few questions about her health: Was she pregnant? Did she have any known chronic diseases? Was there any condition that could make it physically dangerous for her to be paddled? If so, could she prove it? That was all the exam consisted of. The doctor told her to pull up her pants and made a note on a slip of paper. He said she should talk to the clerk before she left. Then he walked out.

Next, a clerical worker came over to speak with her. She gave her a card with the date and time appointed for her paddling, along with a list of instructions and the admonishment that any deviation from the printed instructions would result in extra blows.

She was asked to read the instructions aloud and sign them. She kept a copy of the rules, along with the address, date and time set aside for her punishment.

The rules read:

1. Be on time.
2. Wear underwear.
3. Do not use drugs or alcohol before the punishment.
4. Park in Lot B. Pay for your own parking. We do not validate.
5. Check in with the Desk Sergeant and get your paddle from him.
6. Do not set your paddle down until you are called into the punishment room. Then you may set it down long enough to remove your pants.
7. Fold your pants neatly and place them on the chair where you had been sitting.
8. Leave your underwear on and pick up the paddle, go into the punishment room and hand it to the punishment officer.
9. Do not talk in the waiting room.
10. Do not swear at the punishment officer.
11. When called into the punishment room, go in promptly without undue delay.
12. Follow all orders from the punishment officer.

"I thought it would be n... " She fumbled for the words.

"Well, you just have to wait your turn." The clerk had a snotty attitude. "Don't be so damned eager."

"I'm not, believe me. I just thought it would happen now." She didn't like the idea of waiting. "Before I chicken out. I just wanted it to be over with."

"Part of the punishment is the wait, the fear of the pain to come," the clerk said without emotion.

"I'm so scared," Diana swallowed hard. "I'm probably imagining it's worse than it really is."

"No way," the clerk smiled an evil smile. "The pain is far beyond your imagination. I just wish I could be there to see you get it."

"Two days! I'll be a basket case by then," Diana muttered more to herself than this obnoxious woman.

"Well, anticipation is part of the fun," the haughty clerk smiled smugly. "At least for us."

"I can tell," Diana shot back, eyes flashing. "What I can not tell you is what a pleasure it is to deal with the likes of you. I'd hate to lie."

"Be sure to follow those instructions exactly," the catty clerk said grinning viciously, "or it doesn't count and you have to go through it all over again"

"Gee, maybe I'll mess up so I can have all this fun twice." Diana took the paper and left the room.

Diana walked out with her legs still shaking. She couldn't believe that she had picked the physical chastisement. She had never been spanked, hit or beaten by anyone. Ever. The very thought terrified and even embarrassed her beyond belief. She had no choice, no real choice. She was short of money and she would lose her job if she went to jail for 60 days.

The night before her punishment appointment, Diana broke up with her boyfriend. The fight was a total revelation to her.

Eric was someone she had only been seeing for a short time. They were still getting to know each other and had not become lovers yet. He had always seemed so concerned with Diana, treating her as if she were special. He was good-looking, tall with brown hair and pale blue eyes. He was also courteous, professional and successful.

That night he showed Diana another side to his character. He called her and basically ordered her to go out with him. He wanted to go to the opera and he'd bought tickets for that night. He got upset when Diana said she wanted to stay home.

"Really, darling, I don't see why we have to stay home tonight," he said in an irritated tone. "You are making too much out of tomorrow."

"I'm sorry, Eric. I'm upset and scared," she told him.

"It's no big thing, really Diana, most kids get spankings from their parents," Eric stated. "If you're going to make such a fuss over this, maybe you should be more careful not to break the speed limit."

"But I've never been spanked," Diana whispered softly, "and this is so much worse. The pain must be terrible."

"I'm sure you will be all right," he said impatiently. "You should get out tonight and enjoy yourself."

"I don't feel like going out, especially to an opera, with everyone dying in the end. I want to stay home and try to relax. You could come over and keep me company."

"I do not want to sit around your dreary apartment and watch television," Eric refused shortly. "There is no way I'm going to let these tickets go to waste just to sit and watch TV."

"I could really use your comfort, Eric." It was as close as she would come to pleading with him.

"No. I am not wasting these tickets. They were very expensive and you're being selfish to ask me to waste them," he said with a cold fury in his voice. "As it is one of them may go to waste unless I can find a suitable escort."

"You can't blame me for the wasted ticket, I wasn't consulted before you bought them!" she pointed out.

"Now, if you wanted to stay home and work off your nervous tension in bed, I might consider it," he said snidely.

"Eric, you are a creep." Diana was angry. "It's bad enough that you don't have any sympathy, but you're trying to use my own fear to seduce me. That's disgusting."

"You're just upset right now, darling. Relax. I'll see you tomorrow and we can do something then." He was still irritated.

"No," she said coldly, "we can't. We are never going to see each, except by accident, again. I'm learning something now. I'm learning that my feelings are simply not important to you. You are not the caring man I thought I knew. It's over. Goodbye

Eric."

"I'm glad I found out how foolish and self-centered you are Diana," Eric said sharply. "If you change your mind and apologize, I may consider taking you back."

"I won't," she said. "Don't ever call me again."

"I hope they beat you bloody, you cold bitch," he said coldly.

"I am sorry Eric." There was something in her tone that sounded almost humble, then she put more force in her voice. "Sorry I ever met you, you bastard!" She slammed down the phone.

Later, she was pleased when she learned from a mutual friend that Eric got a speeding ticket after storming out of her life.

After breaking up with the creep she sat in front of the television not really watching an old movie and sipping a glass of wine. She shed a few tears over the loss of her relationship, but she considered herself lucky to have seen his true colors. She just sat there, alone with her thoughts. She wasn't hungry so she never even ate dinner. She just stared at the television and went to bed early.

Diana slept poorly that night. She tossed and turned all night long. She was so embarrassed by the thought of being paddled that she hadn't told anyone except Eric about it, so she didn't have a friend to try to comfort or reassure her about the upcoming ordeal. She had even lied to her boss about why she needed the day off work.

She woke early and ate a slice of toast and had a cup of coffee. The thought of eating any more made her feel nauseous. She had made arrangements to have the whole day off work, even though her appointed time was two in the afternoon.

She made sure she dressed in loose, comfortable slacks made of soft cotton. She pulled on a peach T-shirt to go with the tan slacks. She brushed her silky blond hair, pulled it into a long ponytail and decided not to wear makeup. She was ready to go. She left early so she would be sure to get to the police station on time, without having to risk speeding. That wasn't even her biggest fear. Even if she did not get a ticket on the way, any tardiness meant that you would have to face an equal punishment the next day. Failure to show up at all meant that the violator would be arrested, jailed and given a paddling every day for a week. To avoid any problems, she was over a half-hour early.

She parked in the assigned lot and sat there. She took a few deep breaths to gather her courage, and got out and locked her car. She had never felt so totally embarrassed, so humiliated or so scared in her life as when she walked into the police station on the appointed day and time. She entered the building and looked around quickly.

Following the written instructions, she walked up to the burley desk sergeant. She presented him with the form bearing her sentence and appointment time. He looked her over with a rude smirk on his face, time stamped her form, then reached under his counter and brought out a heavy, leather paddle. He grinned at her slyly and handed it to her.

"Take it up to the third floor, Room 310, and be quick about it. Get the time stamped on this card in the room. You have five minutes to get there from here. Take a number, sit down and wait, holding the paddle until you are called for your turn. DO NOT PUT THE PADDLE DOWN UNDER ANY CIRCUMSTANCES! Hand it to the punishment officer when he calls your number," he instructed, pointing to the elevator. "And Miss, have a nice day." It was a sneering insult. He watched her walk away, leering at her well-rounded bottom.

She pushed the button and waited for the elevator. As she stood waiting for the elevator, she heard him laugh.

Diana felt even more humiliated now that she had the paddle in her hand. It seemed to weigh a ton and it was so large that there was no way to conceal it. Everyone had to know just why she was there. It seemed, somehow, as if she were nude in a public place. It felt as if everyone knew her private business. Her face felt like it was on fire from her blushes, and she could feel her bottom throbbing with imagined pain.

The chrome doors opened and she got in.

There was a handsome young police officer already in the

elevator. Seeing the paddle, he automatically pushed the button for the third floor.

"Don't worry, Miss. It'll be all right," he said kindly, the first kind voice she'd heard that day. "It's a stupid law, isn't it? Almost primeval."

Diana couldn't bring herself to look him in the eyes even when she heard him speaking to her. She had a vague impression he was very handsome.

"Or Victorian." She managed a faint smile.

"Anyway Miss, don't be so scared. It won't be so terrible," the young officer said kindly. "You shouldn't be so embarrassed either, these days it's happening to almost everyone. All it means is that you were speeding. The damn fool politicians thought they would raise more money from the fines; instead they wind up making less money and sending this country back to the Middle Ages. Or, like you said, Victorian England."

"If it's any comfort to you, they did screen the officers very carefully," he told her, "to make sure they were not especially brutal or sadists. I hope that helps."

"Thanks, Officer." She glanced at him briefly. "I don't know if anything could help."

The young officer pushed the STOP button and gave her a gentle hug.

"You'll be all right." He squeezed her shoulders gently. "Are you okay?"

Diana couldn't find her voice to answer, but she managed to nod her head. He started the elevator again. She felt a little bit better as she got off the elevator. A very little bit better.

She got off at her floor. He stared at her until the doors closed, and the elevator continued up another floor. God! She was so beautiful with that wavy blond hair, those chocolate brown eyes and that incredible shape. He hoped she'd be all right.

She took a deep breath and entered the door marked 310. It was painted a drab, institutional green. There were bars on the windows and hard, straight-backed wooden chairs lining three of the walls. There were four other people already waiting in the small room: three men and one woman. They were all holding paddles like the one Diana had in her hands.

On the fourth wall she saw a time stamp and a number dispenser, like the one at the deli. She walked over, stamped her card, took a number and sat down. She had pulled number 13 and even though she was not superstitious, it seemed like a bad omen.

There was a lighted sign by the wall-mounted television that showed the number 8 made of big red dots. On the wall mounted television screen there was an odd picture.

It was unmistakable; a close up of a pair of nude buttocks, fleshy, pale and quivering, in living color. She thought they were male but there was no way to really be sure. There was no sound. A paddle began to land of the buttocks with stunning efficiency. That was when she realized the sound had not been turned off. It turned out there was indeed sound with the picture. Horribly clear sound. The CRACK of the paddle hitting the pale flesh and the subsequent gasp of the faceless victim was immediately, chillingly clear. It was also extremely intimidating.

Every few seconds a paddle, just like the one she held in her hands, landed on the buttocks with a loud CRACK! The blows caused the skin to redden even more.

None of the people waiting were looking at each other in the face. They were all very purposefully trying to avoid looking up at the television monitor on the wall. None of them were succeeding very well.

She tried not to watch the picture, but it was hypnotic and hard to avoid since she was also trying to avoid looking at the other people in the room. She also tried not to listen but it was impossible to ignore. The sights and sounds coming from the television monitor were all pervasive. CRACK! Each smack of the paddle chilled her to the bone. The fleshy bottom was no longer pale, it was turning bright red, and there were bruises forming!

Diana felt sick at the realization that soon her own punishment would be televised to everyone out in the waiting room. She shuttered violently each time the paddle cracked on someone's bottom.

Eventually the punishment stopped. A door in the side of the room opened. A police officer called out the next number. He was a tall muscular man with sandy brown hair, cut very short, and cold hazel eyes. "NUMBER NINE!"

The lighted sign changed to 9.

The oldest of the men got up slowly, resignedly. He turned out to be a short little guy, maybe about 60, with salt and pepper hair, brown eyes and a little potbelly.

He went over to the officer and said, "Yes sir."

"Take off your pants, fold them and put them on the chair. I'll take your paddle," the officer instructed.

The man obeyed, following the officer's orders as he put his pants on the chair and went through the door into the punishment room. Once again there was no sound. The door opened and a stout man of about forty came out carrying a paddle and a slip of paper. He was wearing a white shirt and boxer shorts. His face was set in a carefully blank mask, but he was flushed. Was it due to anger, pain or embarrassment? He avoided eye contact with anyone in the room and made no comment as he walked over to the chair where his gray suit pants were neatly folded. He set down the paddle and the paper. Then he simply pulled his pants on, fastened the zipper and his black leather belt, picked up the paddle and paper and quickly left the room.

A tall black man came into the room and took a number.

The sound came on again and soon everyone was struggling not to watch the older man's punishment. There were no moans or gasps from him until it was almost over. His stoicism was admirable but it also made the paddling more chilling somehow. The CRACK of the paddle seemed even louder. The regularity of the blows was amazing, almost a perfect rhythm. The last three or four swats brought a gasp from the man, then it was over. The light changed to 10.

Again the door opened, the same officer came out. He called

out, "NUMBER TEN!"

A tough young man of about 20 stood up. He had tattoos and spiked hair. His eyebrow and nose were both pierced. He was swallowing rapidly as he stood up and reluctantly removed his tight jeans. He was having a little bit of trouble peeling his tight jeans off. He wasn't wearing underwear, which was against the instruction sheet. The reason for those instructions was now painfully obvious.

The thought crossed Diana's mind that if she was a man, she'd be more careful about who she let see her naked thing. Especially if there was no more to show off than what the teen punk had. No big deal!

She silently thought it was a shame that a guy with such a small dick also had such a small brain. He had long dirty looking sandy colored hair, brown eyes, a heavy metal band displayed on his t-shirt and a tattoo on his butt that read ironically, "KISS MY ASS."

The young man walked to the door and hesitated. Diana felt no sympathy for him. At the door he had abruptly stopped and started to back away.

He panicked. He began to yell at the officer and turned to try and get away. The officer acted quickly; he pushed a buzzer on the wall and called out for back-up. Two strong looking officers, one male and one female, came to help him. They dragged him into the punishment room

The sight of the young man being dragged away only served to strengthen Diana's resolve to follow all the instructions as well she could. As he was dragged into the room, a few of the people gave a nervous laugh.

Soon the older man came out; his face was red and there were traces of tears in his eyes. He dressed quietly and left. The sound came on.

The paddle cracked down on the buttocks of the young man and his punishment began. It was loud and brutal. The officer seemed to be laying it on harder than before. The boy's bottom was very blotchy and reddened by the time it was over. He yelled throughout the whole proceeding but had sense enough not to swear at the officer.

Diana noticed that a young woman sitting in the waiting room with her also shuttered violently each time the paddle landed on the guy's ass. She caught the young woman's eyes with a wry smile. The young man yelled the loudest of any of the victims so far.

The light changed to 11. The officer came in again and called, "NUMBER ELEVEN!"

The woman stood up. Woman was really stretching it a bit, Diana realized, since she was only a girl. A defiant and terrified teenage girl. Diana hadn't paid attention until the girl stood up. The girl was just about 20. Her long curly blond hair was in her face; she pulled it back revealing expressive blue eyes filled with fear and tears, and covered with too much makeup. Her mascara was already starting to run.

She removed her jeans, folded them and walked towards the door. The girl started to follow the officer when she paused, seemingly frozen in place. Diana silently willed the girl to go in without a fuss. The girl did.

Diana, once again, reminded herself to stay in control and try to act brave. She would try to comply with all the officer's orders. It wouldn't be easy, but if a teenaged girl could do it, so could she. Acting like a frightened fool only to be dragged in there was a far worse prospect. Also, there was probably extra punishment for such behavior, and facing 60 swats was daunting enough.

The door closed. Soon after, the door reopened and the young man came out, tight-lipped and grim. He was sporting a pathetic erection and had tear-filled eyes.

While the man was dressing, struggling to pull tight jeans over a very sore bottom, the officer stuck his head out of the door. He reminded him that because he had forgotten the required dress code, he was to report again tomorrow. He would get another paddling. That was the moment when Diana found out that it was possible for a man to flush and go pale at the same time. It was quite a sight. It was almost as much of a spectacle as

ANOTHER BATCH OF WARM BUNS

watching him pull on those tight jeans, with no underwear, a very
sore bottom and an erection.

Diana wondered faintly why the ones coming out emerged a
few moments after the ones going in.

The young punk finished dressing and left quickly. Diana made
a bet with herself that he would wear loose pants tomorrow. She
was glad she had worn her loosest pair of soft, cotton slacks.

A woman came in and took a number. She was almost fifty,
thin and nervous. She had graying hair, glasses, and was wearing
pale green slacks and a floral print blouse. She took her number
and sat down in one of the empty chairs.

Scenes and sounds of the girl's punishment soon filled the
screen. She screamed violently, cursing the unseen officer
wielding the paddle. The nervous woman squirmed in time with
the sound of the paddle on the girl's bottom. The sounds filled
Diana's soul.

The unseen girl yelled, "You fucking pig!"

The sound went off. After several seconds, it came on again
and the officer said to his unseen audience. "This girl will have
her punishment increased by ten strokes for swearing at me. Let
that be a warning to all of you."

The beating started again but this time the girl screamed
wordlessly.

The light changed to 12. The door opened.

"NUMBER TWELVE!"

Another person came in and took a number, sitting next to
Diana. It was a man. She barely noticed him. Diana swallowed
tightly as a middle-aged man with short, straight, brown hair and
a slim build stood up. He looked to Diana like a businessman,
maybe an accountant. He stood up and removed his pants.

Diana shivered. Her turn was coming! She just wanted to get
through this as well as possible. She really wanted to follow the
instructions to the letter to avoid getting any extra punishment.

The man handed his paddle to the officer, took off his pants
and went through the door without a word.

The girl emerged, crying. Her long dark hair covered her

downcast face as she struggled to put her jeans back on. They were fairly tight, and Diana could tell it hurt the girl to pull them up and fasten the zipper.

A gray-haired woman came in looking extremely frightened. She took a number and sat down. On the screen, the beating of the man began.

From the television monitor came the sights and sounds of the man's punishment. To Diana, every stroke of the paddle seemed to be taunting her.

WHACK! WHACK! Diana knew her turn was next. God! She wanted to run! WHACK! This beating seemed much louder and harder than the ones before it. WHACK! Her heart seemed to jump with every CRACK of the paddle. WHACK! Scenes of the man's harsh punishment filled the screen, and sounds of the punishment filled Diana's senses. WHACK! The only sounds she could hear were the smacks and CRACKs of the paddle, the man's boisterous yells and her own beating heart. The paddling stopped. The door opened.

Her turn was next and she was terrified! The light changed to 13!

The officer called, "NUMBER THIRTEEN!"

Diana swallowed hard and stood up on shaky legs, barely managing to say, "Yes, officer, I'm here."

She stood up quickly, willing herself to act without thinking about anything but the immediate task at hand. She handed her paddle to him. She focused her attention on lowering her zipper then stepping out of her shoes. Sliding one leg out of her slacks, then the other leg. Folding and setting the slacks on the chair.

On trembling legs but with her head held high, she walked through the door with the officer in a confident manner without hesitation. Next, she handed the slip of paper and the paddle to the corrections officer. So far, so good.

The small punishment room was the same drab green as the waiting area. She saw the man who preceded her. He was standing against what looked like a long padded table with some straps on it. His upper body was bent over, and his chest rested on the tabletop. He turned to look at Diana. His face was red, his expression guarded. He had not pulled up his underwear. His buttocks were red and terribly bruised.

She was surprised to notice that he seemed basically decent, with no obvious sarcasm or hostility. He was also good looking, tall and muscular, with close-cropped black hair, blue eyes and a chiseled face. The first thing he did was have her take a Breathalyzer test for the presence of alcohol.

"I have to test for alcohol to make sure you don't dull the pain with liquid anesthetic," the officer said frankly. "If you were legally drunk, we'd send you home and reschedule you for a double dose another day." He quickly checked the results.

"You passed." The officer ordered her to look closely at the man's bruises, and to touch the man's buttocks to feel the heat coming from them.

It was then that she realized why the businessman was still in the room standing in place, looking somber and pale.

"That's how your butt will look and feel in just a few minutes," he said to her. His voice was cold and utterly without emotion. "Now pull up his underwear."

Diana did as she was told, gingerly pulling up the stranger's underwear. Next, at the officer's direction the other man moved away from the table.

"Ma'am, walk over to the whipping bench and stand up against it at the end," the officer said without any trace of emotion. "This gentleman will strap you in place."

Diana complied reluctantly, of course. Soon she was standing at the end of the table, trembling with fear. Tears were already streaming down her face, and she was afraid that her legs would not support her. She stood there without moving while the man who had been paddled came up behind her and, with trembling fingers, lowered her lacy nylon underwear down to her feet uncovering her butt. That was the hardest and bravest thing Diana had ever done.

The officer went on with his instructions. At his direction, the man used the straps to attach her feet to the legs of the table, keeping her legs wide apart. Next, he moved up to fasten a strap around her upper thighs.

"Bend over, please," he said in a tight voice.

It was almost a relief to be able to rest on the table, almost. She was very conscious of her exposed buttocks sticking out. She felt naked and vulnerable

When she had, he fastened a strap that went across her back, just above the swell of her buttocks. He fastened her hands together, and fastened them to a hook out in front of her head.

She was very uncomfortable as the straps were very tight. Her arms were straining from being stretched, and her full breasts were flattened painfully on the table.

Her discomfort and her discomfiture at being exposed to total strangers only added to her total fear and abject humiliation.

At the officer's nod the man picked up his paddle and his slip of paper, now signed by the officer, and left the room.

"Alone at last," the officer said softly but somehow not unkindly.

The officer flipped a switch. "The television picture is on but there's no sound yet. I want to tell you a few things before we begin. First, I have no choice but to be severe. I'll admit it, we both know that a paddling as severe as this one will be is one hell of a punishment for 10 lousy miles per hour over the speed limit, if you were even really going ten miles over." He paused. "I get monitored and the television monitors are watched by my superiors. If I don't punish you harshly enough or if I fail to live up to their expectations, I get put in your place. I won't be put in that position. Next, yell all you want, but do not swear, especially not at me, since it will increase your punishment." He paused again. "This is painful but you will survive it, and, you won't be really injured. It will take less than two minutes, so hold on and be brave. You can take it. I know you can. Concentrate on your breathing. Any questions?"

She shook her head, unable to speak aloud. "I'm turning on the sound now." He flipped the switch and picked up the paddle. "Take a long, deep breath and hold it, then let it out slowly."

As soon as she had drawn a shaky breath, he said, "Another."

She took another deep breath as he switched on the monitor.

He said, "Again."

She did it.

CRACK! Without any further warning, he swung the paddle and hit her on the butt, very hard. CRACK! She gave a sort of half-gasp, half-scream. It was worse than she imagined. Much worse. CRACK!

CRACK! He hit her again. CRACK! Again. CRACK! And again. The blows fell hard and sure with cold regularity, spaced just over one second apart.

All the blows were given with a heavy hand and absolutely no mercy. All the blows hurt, and they hurt a lot. The paddle was big and wide enough so that each one of the blows landed on both cheeks of her ass.

Each one was harsh and each one hurt, but it was the cumulative effect that was so devastating. Although she had not realized it, the corrections officer tried to spread the swats out all over her bottom. She simply did not have a big enough bottom to handle 60 swats without them overlapping often, so the paddle landed on the same spots over and over.

The longer the harsh punishment lasted and the more swats she received, the more the pain of each loud, hard blow increased.

Diana tried to be silent but all too soon she was gasping aloud at each stroke of the paddle; then she was yelling. Unintelligible words.

She was crying and screaming out loud now. CRACK! The paddle descended again and again on the same sore area. CRACK! Her buttocks felt hot and heavy, as though they were swollen. The relentless paddling continued. CRACK!

Then, in a short eternity, it was over. The punishment ended. The officer stopped hitting her and she stood there with her buttocks throbbing painfully. She was sobbing and tears were running down her face.

"You did well." The officer unstrapped her restraints. He told her to stay in place and not to pull up her underwear.

Impersonally, he handed her a box of tissues before he went out the door to call the next person in line.

Diana stood there with her hands rubbing her backside gently. She was sobbing, hurting, and she really wanted to go home. When the next person, the tall black man, came in, she still laid on the table while he looked at and felt her bruises. She felt him pull her lacy panties back into position. Then she waited for her turn to lower his underwear and fasten him into the required position. After she had done so, the officer pointed to the door and told her she could leave. He handed her a signed paper, her proof that her punishment was really, finally, over.

Diana went back to the waiting room, put on her pants, and carrying the paddle, left the room. She took the elevator down and went to the desk sergeant. She had to give him one copy of her paper and return the paddle.

This time when she went to the front desk she saw the police officer who had been in the elevator with her. He gave her a warm, sympathetic smile, took her paddle and her paperwork, and treated her with courtesy in every way. He was also extremely handsome.

"Are you okay?" he whispered, sounding genuinely concerned.

He had short dark hair, deep brown eyes, a muscular build and a face to die for!

She took a deep breath and managed a weak smile as she answered his question. "Well, I don't recommend it for laughs, but I think I'll live."

There was still a trace of pain in her eyes, and the redness from her tears. "Thank you for asking."

He returned part of the form and whispered again, quietly saying, "I know this is probably the last thing that you would like to hear right now but, what the hell, a man's got to take a chance." He smiled at her. "My name is Robert. I'd like to get to know you. Could I come over to see you sometime?"

He admired her soft, brown eyes and her long, silky, blond hair. She had a great figure too.

She was in a great deal of pain and eager to get out of there, but he was so darn good-looking! He seemed really nice too.

"Yeah, I, ah, I guess so," she stuttered out her confused reply. "Someday."

"Great!" He flashed her a smile and said sympathetically, "Try using a cold cloth on the, um, damaged area."

"Okay, goodbye." She left, not even realizing that he had never asked for her address or phone number.

He watched her leave, then following an impulse he'd never had before on the job, he noted her name and address in his small notepad. He got off work in two hours. He couldn't, could he?

Diana was very uncomfortable on the drive home. Her car had been sitting in the afternoon sun and the seat was hot. Her underwear chafed. Her loose comfortable slacks felt too tight, and the soft cotton fabric seemed rough and scratchy. The plush car seat seemed too hard. Her bottom stung and ached. She just wanted to get inside her apartment and lie down, face down.

Once she was in her apartment, she took a cool shower to refresh herself. She put on a soft cotton sleep shirt, like an extra large T-shirt, with pictures of flowers and butterflies on it, and no underwear.

She didn't just use a cold cloth, she used an ice pack. Somehow in spite of her pain, she managed to find a position on the sofa that wasn't too uncomfortable, and lay on the sofa listening to a soft rock station on the stereo.

She was vaguely wondering what she would have for dinner, but it seemed too much of an effort to get up and fix something. She ached, but worse than that was the pain of the humiliation she'd felt all during the paddling. Everything from the front desk Sergeant, to the waiting room with the television, to having a stranger strap her down had been like an extra punishment, over and above the paddling.

She had to admit though, the officer who actually paddled her could have been worse. True to what she'd been told in the elevator, he didn't seem to be sadistic or unnecessarily cruel, just coldly efficient. And the officer from the elevator, the one who had been at the desk as she left, was terrific. He had been warm and friendly, with real sympathy and understanding in his smile. He was also, and she was forced to remember, very handsome!

She allowed herself to savor the memory of his warm brown eyes and his genuine friendly smile. His description sounded so average: Short brown hair, brown eyes, six foot tall, strong but not stocky build. Firm, even features, with full lips, a chiseled chin and a dimple on one cheek that showed when he smiled. That description fell short of capturing the essence of the man, his warmth and concern. It also fell far short of describing how very handsome he was. The only good thing to come out of the ghastly day. She'd probably never see him again, just her luck.

Almost the moment she had that thought her doorbell rang. "Who is it?" she called, almost defiantly. She did not want company

She sighed as she got off the sofa and winced as the movement made her behind ache again. She went to the door, praying that her ex-boyfriend, the jerk of the western world, wasn't on the other side. She sighed as she looked through the spy hole. It wasn't Eric.

She was shocked to see Officer Wilson standing in her hallway. He was dressed in jeans and a faded blue T-shirt. He was also holding a pizza and a six pack of beer.

"It's Robert Wilson, from the police station. Remember I asked if I could come over?" he called through the door.

"I thought you meant sometime off in the future, not tonight! I'm, uh, not really feeling up to visitors right now. Could you come back another time? Please?"

Although she thought he was cute and she might like to see him again, it had been a rough day, to say the least.

"Open the door, Diana," he said softly but firmly. "Then if you want me to leave, I'll go."

"I really don't feel like company, Officer," she said softly as she opened the door to talk to him.

"I'm sure you don't," he said cheerfully, his dimple showing as he smiled. "Look, I know you're in pain. I can only imagine how badly it hurts, but I thought maybe I could take your mind off things for a while. I was hoping that maybe I could help to cheer you up. Please, give me a chance at least. Do you really want to be alone right now, or are you just embarrassed?" He played his trump card. "I also thought you might not feel like cooking, so I brought pizza and beer."

He made no move to enter. He just leaned casually against her door jab and smiled at her. "I know it's really unprofessional for me to come to your home like this, so if you want me to I'll leave. You can even keep the pizza. It's pepperoni with extra cheese, by the way. I'd really like to come in for a while though."

It worked! The idea of pizza won her over; she was very hungry, she realized.

She opened the door wider. "You're right, I'm just embarrassed I guess." She considered a moment, then made a gesture at her sleep shirt. "Okay, give me a minute to get dressed and I'll let you come in."

"Don't put on anything special just for me, you're decently covered and you're comfortable, besides I like that butterfly," he said softly, indicating the front of her shirt before walking into the apartment. "I'm not going to take advantage of you. I promise. Besides the pizza's getting cold!"

She took his word for it and decided not to put on anything else. When she opened the door and let him in, she took a long look at him. He had kind eyes and a well-muscled body. He was wearing tight jeans and a blue polo shirt. He came in with the beer and pizza.

"I hope it's all right coming over tonight because I was worried about for you. I didn't think you should be alone and of course, I didn't think you would want to cook or go out to dinner," he smiled at her.

"I know. I'll get some paper plates and napkins," she offered. "Please, sit down"

"No, don't play hostess, just point me to the kitchen so I can get plates and napkins, then you can lie down on the sofa while I wait on you."

She grinned and pointed. "Sounds like a deal to me! The paper plates and napkins are in the kitchen." She laid down on the sofa and waited for him to bring the food.

"I'm sure I'll be able to find whatever we need. You just relax. Do you like to watch football?"

She laughed. "Just like a man. No, I rarely watch football, but go ahead and put the game on. I have a new rule: Anyone who brings me pizza and beer can watch the game "

"Wise rule, Miss." He put down the pizza and went into the kitchen. He put the beer into the refrigerator, keeping two bottles out, then faced the sink and said, "Where would I find paper plates?" He pointed at a cabinet. "Here?" He turned and pointed in another direction. "Or here?"

"Face the first cabinet, then go one door over. No. Left." She watched as he opened the door. "There. Paper plates and napkins. Also, would you please bring me a glass? It's at the back of the cabinet to the right."

He brought out the plates, napkins and a glass for her beer. He handed her a slice of pizza and poured a beer for her. Then he sat on the floor beside her, leaning back against the sofa and clicked the television over to the football game. He left the sound audible but low, and picked up his slice of pizza.

"Miss?" He looked up at her. "May I call you Diana?"

She had just bitten into her slice of pizza so there was a pause before she answered. When she did she spoke very seriously. "Please. You're sitting on my floor eating pizza and drinking beer, while watching football and I'm only half dressed. I think you should call me Ms. McKinny."

It was a pretty cold bluff, but the sparkle in her eyes gave her away. "Great then, you can call me Officer Wilson," he shot back.

"Thank you for the pizza, Robert," she said softly.

"My pleasure, Diana," he smiled at her. "Isn't this better than sitting here alone?"

"It sure is." She savored the pizza.

It felt like it was just what the doctor ordered, as her dear old mum used to say. She seldom drank beer, but it seemed perfect with the pizza.

Her doorbell rang. "I'll get it if you'd like."

At her nod, Robert got up and went to the door. He looked through the spy hole, then opened the door.

"May I help you?" he politely asked whoever was there.

"I can see it sure didn't take her long to replace me," Eric said in a hurt tone.

"Obviously not," Robert said dryly. "Why would it?" He shut the door as Eric left.

"Who was it?" Diana asked him.

"He didn't give a name, but he said something about you finding a replacement quickly." It was a question.

"That would be Eric then," she said, shaking her head. "We broke up last night. He said I was selfish because I didn't feel like going to the opera. I was scared and upset and he didn't even seem to care. I just upset his plans. Plans he made without even consulting me, I might add."

"He didn't realize you were worried and upset?" Robert was amazed. "That should have been one of those nights where your feelings took top priority. I mean, I'm sure there are some nights when you would put his feelings first, and of course there are some nights when your entitled to have him think of taking care of you."

"That's what I thought," she admitted. "But apparently, I was supposed to go along with whatever he wanted."

They sat there companionably eating pizza. He made an occasional comment to the football players, but most of his attention was focused on her.

Robert had just finished his half of the pizza and taken the empty box out to the kitchen when the doorbell rang again. He brought out two more beers, sat them on the coffee table and went to answer the door again.

All she heard him say was, "You snooze, you lose buddy. Thanks." He shut the door with a bang. "It was nobody." He had another six pack in his hands.

Diana was not stupid. "I suspect it was somebody. Who?"

"It was a police officer," Robert admitted, "who wanted to offer you comfort."

"And pizza?" she asked. "Is that the regular thing?"

"No, he had fried chicken," he grinned. "I took his beer." Robert sat down again and opened his beer.

Diana also opened a beer and poured it into a glass. It gave her some time to think. "Pizza's better." She paused, studying his handsome face. "May I ask you a question? I mean a question that you might consider rude?"

"Sure." He was curious.

"I know it's a rotten thing to ask, but a girl can't be too careful." She paused. "How do I put this? Do you do this often? I mean, do you offer comfort to women, ah, after they've been paddled?"

"I've never done it before, but some of the other guys do. Some of the female officers too. Pick up men, I mean. Like I said this is a first for me, but when I saw you I had to give it a try for once," he answered seriously. "You looked so beautiful and scared in the elevator, but also brave. I really wanted to get to know you so I thought it was worth a try. Are you offended?"

"I'm the first, honest?" The thought pleased her.

"You're the first, honest," he smiled at her. "Are you mad?"

"No, of course not," she said. "You've been a perfect gentleman. And I was attracted to you as well. But my next question is harder: Do you plan on doing this again, with some other woman?"

"I can't imagine it," he said with complete honesty. "I think you're one of a kind."

"That's good," she grinned. "I had enough trouble paying the penalty for a traffic ticket, and I'd hate to have to pay the penalty for a murder."

He laughed. "I guess I've been warned."

She grinned back at him. "I guess you have."

He reached his arm up and pulled her down to him for a soft

kiss.

That first kiss was memorable as there was tenderness, plus a surprising amount of heat for a soft kiss. It was not the usual first kiss. It quickly turned into several soft kisses, which grew deeper and longer. They sat there with the game on, but not following the action. Instead they talked.

They finished off the first six pack of beer and just talked. He glanced at the game from time to time noting the score, but except for a touchdown in the final minute of the fourth quarter, the football game was forgotten.

Diana almost choked on her beer when Robert said in a casual tone, "I'd better take a look at your bruises and make sure you're not hurt too seriously."

"You'd better not!" She was indignant.

"Just to be careful, not for any perverted thrill." He reached up to her neck and pulled her head down, but he didn't give her the kiss she expected. Instead, he put his mouth next to hers and asked, "Do you really think that I would want to look at your bruises just as an excuse to try to get into your panties?"

She laughed and said, "Yes! It wouldn't work though."

"Why not?" he asked.

She raised her eyebrows, biting her bottom lip. "No panties." The short phrase was full of mischief.

He kissed her at last, thoroughly. She rolled over and lay on the sofa face down, and he gently raised the bottom of her long t-shirt and examined the bruises. She buried her flaming face in the sofa pillows.

"It's not too bad."

"But what about the bruises?" she asked.

"There's about three dark ones and several faint bruises. Only one of the dark ones looks serious." He stroked it gently. "Right here."

"Oh yeah, I can feel that spot, even without anything touching it. There's an ache with it. And I bet I can tell where the other two dark ones are as well." She lifted herself up on one elbow and looked back at him. "Well Doc, what's the verdict, will I live?"

There was a pause before he answered. In a tight voice he said, "Yes, I think you will with enough tender loving care. It's a very pretty ass, by the way. It probably would look even better without the Technicolor touches."

"Thanks." She turned her head enough for a kiss.

"Want to know a secret?" he asked slowly.

"Sure." She was intrigued. "What's up?"

"I got a speeding ticket driving here tonight," he said in a low voice.

"What?" She was astonished.

"I got a traffic ticket tonight," he repeated. "I wanted to get changed, pick up the pizza and get over as quickly as I could. I was just driving a... "

"A few miles over the limit," she interjected knowingly.

"Why in the heck couldn't it have been the jerk that was at the desk when I first went in? I mean, you're really nice and he was a sarcastic creep! Will you have the same, uh, options I did?" She was wide-eyed.

"Exactly. I'll need to make the same choice you did. God! It will be so embarrassing to be paddled by someone I work with." He didn't look forward to it. "Will you come to see me, um after?"

"Deal. I'll be happy to return the favor," she laughed, giving him a wink. "I'll look forward to it. I owe you one."

"Gee, thanks a lot."

"Funny, I thought cops didn't get traffic tickets. Professional courtesy."

"Me too," he laughed. "But the officer who stopped me didn't seem to realize that. He had no sympathy at all. In fact, he thought it was even worse that a cop, like myself, was speeding.".

The subject was dropped when he kissed her. The kiss developed into a continuous friendly battle of tongues, a gentle duel with no losers. The football game was forgotten as they gave themselves over to the sheer pleasure of kissing each other.

When they stopped to take a deep breath, they both noticed

that the game was over. Robert turned off the television and put on the stereo, and they cuddled for awhile and kissed some more.

Standing up, he said, "I'd better leave. I don't want to, but it's getting late and you've had a rough day. By the way, how do you feel?"

"I'm okay, thanks to you. And there have been some bright spots in my day. I really don't want you to leave," Diana grinned. "Besides, you drank most of the beer. You wouldn't want another ticket, one for D. U. I. would you?"

"I'd like to use that as an excuse to ask if I could stay. The thought of another ticket is enough to make me want to tear out my hair, but I'm really okay. I do have to go."

His obvious reluctance piqued Diana's interest. She realized she was unwilling to let him to leave. She only hesitated a split second. "Robert, you do know I'm not the kind of lady who invites a man she hardly knows to stay the night?" she asked him.

"I know you're not." Then he admitted, "I almost wish you were." He turned for the door. "That's why I have to go now. If I stay any longer, I might make a move that you're not ready for." He gazed at her.

"A move?" She shot him a coy smile. "Like this?"

She stood up and took his hand. "Robert, please stay and make love to me." It was a quiet invitation, but there was nothing hesitant or unsure about it.

"That's pretty much the move that I had in mind all right. Are you sure it's what you want?" He was after all, a gentleman.

"If you leave now, I'll just follow you to your house and jump on your bones," she threatened a friendly threat. "Since we're already here, why waste the time?"

"I just love a logical woman," he whispered softly. "I've wanted you since the moment you opened the door."

"Me too," she admitted softly.

"Took you long enough, then," he grinned. "I thought you'd never ask, love. Are you sure you're all right?" At her nod, he lifted her up with his strong arms and nibbled her ear. "Where's your bedroom, love?" he whispered softly; a gentleman he was, a fool he wasn't.

He carried her into the bedroom and let her down to stand next to the bed. He kissed her once, gently, before stepping back one step. His eyes on her, he pulled his T-shirt over his head, revealing an impressive set of muscles on a lean athletic build. Next, he unbuckled his belt, lowered his zipper and stepped out of his jeans. Diana stood and watched appreciatively as he stepped out of his briefs. His penis, fully erect, was impressive.

Diana's sore behind somehow seemed to add to the sensations she was feeling.

He stepped towards her and raised the sleep shirt over her head. They stood kissing with passion and tenderness for a moment, then without a word they turned together and pulled back the hand-made comforter on the bed.

"Diana, I didn't come prepared," Robert said suddenly. "I didn't dare hope… "

"I'm on birth control," she said softly. "And I've been tested recently against STD's. I believe I'm safe."

"I get tested frequently; not because I sleep around but because I come into contact with HIV infected people everyday at work. I'm always careful. I believe I'm safe too."

"Good enough for me." She got into the bed and reached up for him, ignoring the ache in her behind.

"Are you sure?" he whispered. He went down onto the bed, onto her.

"God. Yes!" She brought her mouth up to devour his and passion exploded with an urgency that left them both breathless.

His mouth trailed down her lovely, round breasts and he suckled them, first one then the other. She writhed with delight and arousal. His mouth trailed lower still, and she moaned in ecstasy. After her climax, he returned to her mouth kissing her deeply.

"My turn," she grinned at him, and she began to explore his body. Following much the same path on his body that he had on hers, she teased and licked at his nipples while her hands caressed and stroked his muscular chest. Her hands trailed lower, to grasp

177

and fondle his large erect penis. Her mouth followed.

He could stand it no longer, he wanted to be inside her. He pulled her head up and kissed her as he plunged into her. There was a moment of acceptance, of welcoming, as her body surrounded his, then the rhythm and movement of loving began.

The lovemaking that night was glorious as there was no awkwardness, no hesitation, no shyness. Her sore bottom was quickly forgotten. The remnants of pain only provided extra sensation as she was transported to a special place with Robert. It was a place of soaring magic and tingling nerve endings, filled with sensations and magic, and good hard multiple orgasms.

Not that she needed any extra sensation while making love with Robert. He turned out to be a fantastic lover who knew instinctively when to be gentle and when to get a little rougher. Was it possible that they had just met?

Something was conceived that night. Oh not a baby, that would come later. What was conceived was a couple who grew to stand together as a single unit. A couple who faced life together. By the time Robert was paddled they were living together. Within a month after that, they were married. They moved away from that town when Robert got a better job offer as an officer on the police force of another city.

But that night the future was still far off. That night, their first night, the fires were even hotter, the passion greater, and the lovemaking was repeated over and over, until they were both exhausted.

Later that night during one of the breaks in the marathon of lovemaking, they curled up together and talked quietly. They learned that they had a lot in common; similar interests in books, movies, and some common views on the world in general. There were differences, but they were not major differences. They also planned to go to the beach the next day. It should be a perfect day, warm and sunny.

Finally Robert brought up a subject that was teasing the back of his mind. "Diana, I've only worked the front desk since they've had paddlings. I've never worked upstairs. Would you please tell me what it's like being paddled? I mean, I know it hurts, but how do they do it? I've never actually seen it done."

She told him. Almost everything.

He was amazed and horrified. "They make us wait? We have to take a number? Remove our pants in front of everyone else in the waiting room? Get strapped down by a stranger, a civilian?" he expostulated. "God! That's barbaric!"

She was glad she hadn't mentioned the closed circuit television and the monitor in the waiting room. She also left out that the stranger also lowers your underwear. Some things you just had to leave for a surprise!

This one was hard to write. It's the only story so far where neither partner is into spanking and that's hard to do in a spanking book! Maybe they'll decide they like it too, we'll have to visit these two in the future. I deserve a treat! I deserve a spanking! Please!

Author's Note

I hope you've enjoyed reading this book. I have two other books that feature some of these characters and some new ones too:

The Paddle Club
a fun, romantic and erotic spanking novel

Hot Crossed Buns
my first collection of short spanking stories

Lately the characters from those books have been depressingly good, but knowing that crew – they'll be in trouble soon, and deserve more spankings.

I also have the romance novel *The Heart Of The Beast*, which has several spankings in it.

www.ingramcontent.com/pod-product-compliance
Lightning Source LLC
Chambersburg PA
CBHW030506260626
47157CB00005B/1669